BLUE EYED STRANGER

ALEX BEECROFT

RIPTIDE PUBLISHING

Riptide Publishing
PO Box 6652
Hillsborough, NJ 08844
www.riptidepublishing.com

This is a work of fiction. Names, characters, places, and incidents are either the product of the author's imagination or are used fictitiously. Any resemblance to actual persons living or dead, business establishments, events, or locales is entirely coincidental.

Blue Eyed Stranger
Copyright © 2015 by Alex Beecroft

Cover art: Lou Harper, louharper.com
Editors: Sarah Frantz Lyons, KJ Charles
Layout: L.C. Chase, lcchase.com/design.htm

All rights reserved. No part of this book may be reproduced or transmitted in any form or by any means, electronic or mechanical, including photocopying, recording, or by any information storage and retrieval system without the written permission of the publisher, and where permitted by law. Reviewers may quote brief passages in a review. To request permission and all other inquiries, contact Riptide Publishing at the mailing address above, at Riptidepublishing.com, or at marketing@riptidepublishing.com.

ISBN: 978-1-62649-213-4

First edition
April, 2015

Also available in ebook:
ISBN: 978-1-62649-212-7

BLUE EYED STRANGER

ALEX BEECROFT

RIPTIDE PUBLISHING

*To my therapist, with whose help I've been fighting my own depression.
And to my husband who loves me even at my worst.*

TABLE OF CONTENTS

Chapter 1	1
Chapter 2	11
Chapter 3	17
Chapter 4	23
Chapter 5	31
Chapter 6	37
Chapter 7	45
Chapter 8	49
Chapter 9	53
Chapter 10	59
Chapter 11	69
Chapter 12	75
Chapter 13	83
Chapter 14	91
Chapter 15	99
Chapter 16	113
Chapter 17	125
Chapter 18	133
Chapter 19	139
Chapter 20	147
Chapter 21	155
Chapter 22	163
Chapter 23	171
Chapter 24	179
Chapter 25	187

CHAPTER ONE

"I am Hasheput! Tremble before my mighty sword!"

Martin Deng detached himself from the shelter of the school's back porch to watch tiny Trisha Nkembe flourishing her badminton racket like a legendary weapon of yore. She had an army of five followers, their scowly-faced seriousness a little belied by the plastic bobbles in their hair. They were facing off the dastardly Ammonites, led by Oscar Peterson in a bucket helmet liberated from the gym equipment storage room.

Martin smiled and walked into the standoff, where he was eyed with resentment and trepidation, and one cry of "I never did nothing!" from Natalie Hoon in the back.

"We don't mean no harm," Trisha got out, preempting his teacherly wrath. "We ain't going to have a real battle. It's a peace talk, right? Because they know already that Queen Hasheput is gonna smash their heads in if they try anything."

The combination of defiance and enthusiasm warmed his heart. "Oh, no," he said, before he could spoil their playtime entirely. "That's fine. It's just that her name is Hatshepsut, which is a little harder to say but worth it, don't you think? And it's not a sword; it's a mace."

"What's a mace, sir?"

"It's like a big club." He gestured. "Like a baseball bat, but made of stone. You really would be able to smash people's heads in with it."

"Whoa, cool!"

"Just—" he backed off with a hand gesture that gave the breezy May lunchtime back to them "—checking your historical accuracy. Might as well get it right, right? Carry on, then."

A real punch-up across the other side of the playground caught his eye, making him turn and stride away to break it up, but he did it with an internal smile. It was great to see the kids responding to history with such enthusiasm. Great to see the way they bloomed when they realized that the world was full of heroes *just like them*.

He relived the memory of Trisha's head coming up, her eyes widening, as he told them about the Nubians in Egypt. When he first took over the class, she had been one of those students who laid their heads on their arms, draped over their desks like the dead.

He knew how she felt. The teaching of history in UK schools could so easily be an all-white thing. Not a deliberate glorification of the Anglo-Saxon race, nothing as egregious as that, but simply the underlying assumption that all the important things in world history had been done by white people, whether those people were British or Roman.

Trisha's astonishment when he began to put up images that proved there had been people of colour in Britain since Roman times, and that people of colour had had a long and glorious history in the world, had been echoed all over the class. Children who'd picked up the modern myth that all black people had once been slaves, and who therefore had rejected history as something they didn't want to know about, suddenly began to see themselves as kings and prophets and world leaders.

It was Martin's magic. Once he'd seen the transformation in his black kids, he'd hunted down little-known facts for the children of other ethnicities, and for the girls. Through warrior queens, pioneer aviators, the Night Witches of the Second World War, and the pirate empire of Ching Shih, he had taught his girls that they too could be glorious. Now they came into his class prepared to be amazed and inspired. They came with their heads up and their little faces bright, reassured of their own noble heritage and potential.

And apparently it spilled out onto the playground too.

After dealing with the scrap before anyone got a bloody nose, he handed off the playground watch to Mrs. Hobbs, the chemistry teacher, so that he could retire to the staffroom and get some lunch.

Satisfaction carried him buoyantly through corridors whose yellowed paint was pocked all over with the greasy spots of Blu-Tack. The macaroni art of the junior school wing gave way to the informational posters of the GCSE curriculum as he swung past the ground floor toilets, up two flights of stairs, and into the attic room the teachers had claimed for their own.

Mr. McKay, the PE teacher, looked up from his Tupperware container of quinoa salad to say, "All right?"

"Pretty good," Martin agreed, putting the kettle on for a cup of tea and a pot of instant noodles. "You ever thought of teaching them fencing? They don't know the first thing about real armed combat."

McKay laughed, and gave him the *you're a weirdo but you seem harmless* expression he so often got when he forgot himself and talked about his obsessions. "Well now, I would have said that was a good thing. Actually, I think sports were invented to replace the use of lethal weaponry among our schoolchildren."

Early summer sunshine slanted into the room through the windows at the eaves and heated up the old sofas and the paint. With the advent of the hot dust smell he associated with summer, his mind turned to the weekend. The first show of the season.

It was Friday, and freedom was only three hours away. And there were so many things he still had to do.

The kettle switched itself off. "Yeah," Martin said, tipping water on his lunch and filling the air with a smell like Marmite. "But you have to force them to do games. I bet they'd be queuing up for sword fighting, and it's good exercise."

McKay looked at him sideways from beneath his sandy lashes. "You're itching to get away, aren't you? Got one of your events this weekend?"

"How could you tell?" In Martin's day, PE teachers had been nasty, small-minded little martinets. He was always thrown when McKay said something insightful.

McKay laughed again. "Any time you start talking about sword fighting, I know you're due in on Monday bruised and hungover and stinking of smoke."

Martin found himself by the window, gazing out over car parks and the backs of the suburban streets, tapping on the glass. He wasn't sure if McKay's comment had provoked his impatience, or if it had been simmering all day, simply interrupted by the satisfaction of having something he'd taught finally sink in.

"Well, it would be good if I *could* get away." Articulating the sentiment seemed to make it worse. "I've got a show over in Trowchester that opens at nine o'clock tomorrow morning. Which means I've got to get the car packed and drive over there tonight..."

And I have to unpack when I'm there, and set up my tent and the work shelter, and find the people in charge of providing sand and wood for the firebox, and locate the standpipes for water. Which will inevitably not be turned on yet. And hunt down the guy responsible to get him to turn them on. And fill the water barrels, and haul them from tap to tent. And cut up the wood because it will be too thick. And inflate my mattress. And locate a shop where Edith can buy fresh milk and bread. And...

Fucking organisers who wanted their shows open first thing in the morning had *no idea*. If he had to spend all day at school first, he'd be doing all of it in the dark, working flat out until midnight or later. He'd start the weekend exhausted and cranky, and it would only go downhill from there.

"I've actually only got one lesson scheduled for this afternoon," he ventured.

McKay snorted, and rose to check the timetable pinned on the corkboard by the fridge, above the dozens of used tea bags heaped on the empty foil takeaway container. "I... happen to be free at that time. But I don't know shite about history."

Tempting. Very tempting. "I... uh. I have a programme about the Air Transport Auxiliary I've been meaning to show them for the Second World War module. If you were kind enough to take over for me, all you'd need to do would be to wheel the TV in and switch it on."

McKay put his whistle between his teeth and gave him a double thumbs-up. "But you'll owe me. Next sports day, you'll be my second-in-command."

Martin rolled his eyes as though he were very put-upon, but couldn't help grinning, immensely relieved. This would help so much. "It's a deal."

His back was to the door, and his nose in his plastic pot of noodles as he slurped them down. He didn't register there was something wrong until McKay straightened up, tucked his whistle inside his shirt and gave him the urgent side-eye of doom.

Only then did he hear the faint creak of leather shoes and scent the Old Spice aftershave of the Head's PA, standing silently, judgmentally, directly behind him.

Glossy was the word that came to mind when Martin contemplated the Head's personal assistant. One of the new breed of young men who spent more time than pageant queens beautifying themselves. Charlie's carefully cropped red hair had a curling spiral shaved above one ear. There was a gold ring in his left eyebrow, but from the neck down he was plastic perfect, as though he had spent his lunch hour pressing his slacks and starching the points of his collar.

"Mr. Deng. The Head would like a word with you."

Martin's good mood took a nosedive, as though the engines had cut out catastrophically on both wings. "I'll be right along. Let me just . . ." He waved his fork to illustrate the inch of noodles and the half cup of tea he had left to consume.

"Of course." A cold smile, too indifferent to be called hostile, and the PA departed.

"I hear tell he files his socks on the Dewey Decimal System," McKay murmured sympathetically, "and only goes home to plug himself into the wall to recharge."

The noodles had in fact lost their appeal. Martin pinched the foil cover back in place over the top of the tub and dumped them in the bin. "What have I done now, I wonder?"

"One way to find out."

The school was laid out on a roughly cruciform pattern, all four corridors coming together to form a central hub. Here, the desks of the school's administrative staff surrounded the inner sanctum of the Head's office. Martin waved to Maureen on reception, but she was too busy trying to puzzle out a spreadsheet—nose pressed to the computer screen—to acknowledge him.

Going past, he stopped outside the white-painted door in the white-painted wall, retucked his T-shirt into his trousers, and smoothed down his jacket sleeves.

The door sat ajar in its frame. Snatches of voices filtered through the crack. Martin stepped up to knock, and heard the gravelly alto of the Head's voice scoff, "I even heard he might be gay."

5

He froze midmovement. His heart stilled and his ears strained to hear more. Charlie was saying something now, but it was too smooth, too low-key to make out.

"Well, one doesn't want that kind of person in charge of vulnerable children."

The air around Martin burned away in a short-lived inferno of rage, and when it was gone, fear rushed in to fill the gap. He loved this job, this school, but damn, he despised the Head, and she . . . well she obviously returned the sentiment. But she couldn't do anything. Even if she did find out he was gay—and God knew how she would do that when he hadn't had time for a relationship in the last three years—she couldn't fire him for it. He would take it to an employment tribunal. He would win.

And then everyone would know.

He swallowed, all the joy of the playground gone beyond recall. He wasn't ready for anyone to know. Not yet. Not with his father already disappointed he was a jobbing teacher and not a professor. Not with his mother already blaming herself for his sister's depression, certain to blame herself for this too.

Queasy, seasick from being tossed between anger and dread, he pushed the door open without knocking and went in.

". . . don't want to do anything illegal."

The door bounced off the rubber stop screwed into the blue carpet. Charlie fell silent and turned to look at him, pulling the lever arch file he carried closer to his chest.

Behind the desk, the Head placed her pen carefully in its penholder. She had finely coiffed bright silver hair and wore a black polyester blouse printed with white dots.

"Thank you, Charlie."

She indicated the seat across from herself, and as Martin lowered himself into it, Charlie left the room and closed the door behind him.

"Mr. Deng. I won't keep you long. I know you have a lesson coming up in—" she checked her watch, which hung around her neck on a chain like a steampunk pendant "—ten minutes. I presume you know why you've been called here."

"I don't," Martin said curtly. If she was going to insult him, she could damn well have the courage to do it to his face. "I've not been made aware of any problem."

"Oh well, consider this fair warning, then." She smoothed her skirt over her knee and tilted her office chair back to stare out of one of the small windows through which she kept her eye on the surrounding desks. Her pink lipstick matched her nail varnish so perfectly it looked as though she'd lacquered her lips.

Time was suspended for an agonising moment, and then she began to speak. "I'm afraid, Mr. Deng, that your performance is subpar. I'm going to have to insist on some changes in future. Firstly, this is a school into which parents compete to place their children. Your appearance should reflect that. This—" she gestured at his clothes "—is unacceptable."

He could see that, he supposed. Truth was, he'd put on something this morning that he would be able to load the car in. The work shelter was coated inside with soot, the cooking equipment coated with it outside, so he was wearing a black Metallica T-shirt, and perhaps he should have gone the extra step and added *Get changed into camping tat* to the long list of things he had to do this evening.

Acknowledging the fairness of her point, he nodded, chastened and not liking the feeling very much.

"Your timekeeping leaves a great deal to be desired."

The weight in his stomach sank a little lower. Looked like she had a point there too. "I'm sorry?"

"Unpaid leave is for emergencies, Mr. Deng. Not so you can drop your responsibilities here whenever your bizarre hobby calls you."

Guilt began to tip back into anger again. "That's not fair. I don't do it that often. It's been, what? Three times this year so far."

"Three times this year and we are barely into May." She levelled her chair off and skewered him with a gaze that was like an icicle driven through the eye. His lips went cold. "Last year it was twice before May, seven times over the summer, another three over the autumn term. I note therefore that it's escalating. There is little point in retaining a teacher who can't be bothered to be here."

"Bretwalda is young," Martin said defensively. "My reenactment society, that is. This year is important for it to establish itself. But when it *has*—when it's properly up and running—I'll be able to ease back and let other people do some of the work."

The Head looked at him as though he had been trying to explain how the dog had eaten his homework. "The troubles of your private life do not concern me. I need to know that when you are employed by this school, you will actually be available to this school. I expect more from my team, Mr. Deng. I expect commitment, and I'm not sure you have it."

"That's a bit rich. I spend *hours* at home, fact-checking the curriculum, figuring out how it can be tweaked to make it interesting and affirming for my class. I'm utterly committed to—"

The Head raised her painted-on eyebrows at him. "And that," she snapped, her voice so frigid it was a wonder the particles of dust in the air didn't precipitate as snow, "that is my third point. Mr. Deng..."

It was really beginning to annoy him the way she kept referring to him. *Yeah, that's my name. Don't wear it out.*

"I must insist that you return to teaching the curriculum as it is set. No more of these wild forays into the realms of the outré. You're giving the children a false impression of the past. A parade of freaks and exceptions do not constitute history."

Martin had taken the other two points relatively calmly, since they reflected on nobody but himself. Touching this one was like touching a match to petrol. He filled up with so much fire he could feel it squeezing out through his pores.

"'Official' history—" Martin curled his fingers in the air to make the condemning quote marks plain "—the history they want us to teach, is nothing more than a tool designed to make every one of those kids think that if it's not done by white men, it's not important. You know what I found when I started looking? I found that people of colour had been here all along. We'd been doing amazing things all along, and someone deliberately took that knowledge away. Someone chose to cover those facts up to keep us in our place. I'm not teaching my kids exceptions. I'm teaching them the truth."

He had half risen from his seat, his fingers gripping the edge of the desk tightly as the flip side of Trisha's joy scoured through him. Fury. Because finding out that you'd been here all along also meant finding out that you'd been lied to all this time. Deliberately lied to so you would carry on feeling small and worthless and foreign, so you would feel you had less of a right to be here than your neighbours.

"That's quite enough." The Head had shrunk back into her seat. A shrill note in her voice sobered him up. He hadn't meant to frighten her.

She pulled a lace-edged handkerchief from her pocket and wiped her brow. "This school is in the business of making sure our children pass the exams they will need for their future. Regardless of your opinions on the veracity of the material, you will teach your class the curriculum as it is given to you. Do you understand me?"

Oh yes, he understood. He thought again about Trisha, how her whole soul seemed to light up when she learned of Kandace of Nubia, of Nefertiti, and Hatshepsut. He would welcome an angry woman with a stone mace at his back right now.

Could he do it? Could he teach the pap that was handed down to the kids here as history? Next year, could he watch the new faces stay closed, and live with himself knowing those kids' hearts were withering inside with every iteration of the unspoken message that they weren't interesting enough to make it into the books?

But in this climate of recession, with jobs hard to come by and his father's disappointment like Banquo's ghost at his feast, could he refuse?

Fury blazed and then burned out. He didn't need this right now. He had a show to get organised. The rest of the garrison were depending on him. He could figure this one out later if he could only get away. "I understand."

"Good," she said and smiled at him, driving a nail straight through his heart. "Then you may go."

CHAPTER TWO

Billy didn't notice the light at first, as dark grey slid into pale. Mist pooled in the churchyard and dripped from yews and gravestones alike. Skeins of it floated into the porch and silvered his black trousers with dew. Every so often one of his hands lifted by itself and wiped the damp from a face that was no warmer than the stones on which he sat.

There was no time. He'd left time behind with everything else when he sat down. Since then there had only been the creeping awareness of wet and cold and misery. The night was endless and Billy was captured by it, as dark and chill inside as the star-sprinkled void above.

But now the sun was pushing its curves over the distant street of terraced houses where Billy lived. He could look out and see the footpath pass through the lich-gate, leap over the small runnel of water that moated the church, and widen out to run along parallel to his road. He could see the wall of his back garden with its blue-painted gate, the locked and shuttered windows of the ground-floor flat, and the marigolds in the window boxes of his kitchen.

It was perhaps five hundred yards away. He was a well-fed, healthy young man of twenty-four, and it should be perfectly within his capability to get up, walk over to his back gate, let himself in, and go to bed.

So do it, he thought, gathering his resolve for the thousandth time that night. *Get up. Get up and walk to your house. Get up!*

But he didn't get up. Somewhere between the intention and the action, a gear in his mind failed to mesh with its opposite. The cogs spun, but the clutch was disengaged.

Get up!

He pulled his knees in to his chest and rested his forehead on them. There was a brief billow of cold as the warm air he had generated around him was disturbed. It built up again slowly where he was folded in two, his belly still warmish, though there was no heat in his knees to soothe his numb face.

This was bad. Worse than it had been for a while.

Get up, damn you! Get up before you die of exposure. Get up. Walk home and have a bath. You can do it.

That was a bloody lie. Other people managed to avoid spending the whole night zoned out because they'd reached the end of their strength. Other people had the resilience, the determination, to walk or even crawl to safety, when it was in sight.

But you're not other people. I fucking wish you were, you loser.

Sunlight slid across the graveyard towards him, dissipating some of the mist, making the droplets glitter as they pitter-pattered from the trees. Yew berries glowed like blood spatter among the dark needles, and Billy looked at his cuffs, where the bloodstains were beginning to brown.

He should get up.

They'd called themselves "the beaters," although that wasn't at all accurate. He and Jimmy James and that fellow from the Black Bull, all employed for the day by Lady Harcombe to do the grunt work at a rabbit shoot on her estate.

Billy had inherited his family house when he had to move his mum into the nursing home, his father long dead by that point. He had split it into three flats and kept the middle one for himself. The rent from his tenants now covered most of his bills and necessities, but he picked up work where he could to finance the rest of it—to buy little treats, to pay for lunches at fast-food vans during the summer season's shows. To buy an occasional round, to keep the heating on an extra hour in the winter.

So when Jimmy told him he could pick up sixty pounds for spending a day driving a party of toffs around the fields and woodlands of Harcombe House, he'd gone along like a dog to a walk, tail wagging. And yeah, there'd been something properly satisfying at taking part in such a country task, more or less like his ancestors must have done since Anglo-Saxon times—because when the censors of the Domesday book came to Rosebery Wood, Billy's family had already been there waiting for them.

His mood had matched the bright morning as Mr. Carter, the gamekeeper, had given them a rundown on the task of rabbit hunting. He and Jimmy and Black Bull Man in a respectful row behind the Barbour-clad guns.

"If you're not sure you can get a clean shot to the head, don't try at all," Carter said for the third time. "We want a humane kill. The little buggers are undermining our land, killing our trees, eating the grass that's meant to feed the deer, so they've got to go. That doesn't mean we should be cruel. If you're not confident of your aim, don't shoot. Don't go for any trick shots. There's no bloody glory in bagging two at once if one of them's suffering."

Carter shrugged apologetically. "Rabbit's poor sport, I know, and we'll set up to try for goose tonight, but at this time of year you have to take what you can get. Now gentlemen . . . and your ladyship. To your vehicles."

Billy hadn't expected it to be so easy. His job was to drive a party of three guns on a predetermined route through the gorse and grass of the meadows to the west of the house, swinging round to take in a band of woodland before coming out on the emerald-green lawns that swept up to the great doors.

Rabbits clearly did not recognise cars as a threat. They were lolloping about in the fresh May sunshine, nibbling on the lush grass, grooming their ears, and busying themselves with pressing rabbit concerns, when *pfft* went the silenced .22 rifles, like a man tutting against his teeth, and they fell over, quite silently.

He had braced himself for the shots, but they were quieter than a polite lady's sneeze. The shattering thing was the way some of the rabbits jumped when they had a bullet in their brain. Two feet off the ground, kicking wildly in an electric fit of death. Billy had watched in astonishment the first time, scarcely aware of the little snake of cold that entered his chest at the sight.

"That'll do," Lady Harcombe had called when the field was pockmarked with furry corpses. She caught Billy's uncertain eye. "You can't risk spending too long on one field. If they notice what's going on, next time you come they'll all go underground at the first shot."

He moistened his mouth, swallowed at the thought that this happened regularly, at the thought that the animals were intelligent enough to get scared. "Right."

"Well, off you go and pick them up, then."

Perhaps *that* had been the most shattering thing, come to think of it—the warm paws twitching in his hands, the way the animals jerked as if they were trying to get away from him, though half their heads were gone. The warm spurting blood on his fingers, on his coat, on his cuffs.

Billy hauled himself out of the memory, put his hands between his knees, and felt like a cancer cell in the body of the universe—something that needed to be destroyed. He was a country boy, through and through. How could he be so pathetic as to mind a little blood? Two of those rabbits were in his freezer right now, a bonus on top of his pay, and he was going to eat them. He was. Because what else was meat for?

His dad would be ashamed if he were still alive to see it. His mum, who had raised chickens and wrung their necks when the time came, would also be ashamed. Billy was ashamed.

He was ashamed, and that was why he couldn't get up.

But it wasn't the only reason. After all, he had got himself back from the shoot okay, put the rabbits in the freezer, and started making lunch with something like a normal person's aptitude. The church bells were the real culprit.

Billy had checked his watch while he waited for his toast to pop and found out he was already ten minutes late for his regular slot showing the tourists around Rosebery church. He'd just turned the flames out under the beans in the pan and left.

Generally he enjoyed the church, enjoyed showing visitors around it, explaining the differences between the very earliest Saxon stonework with its mock-wooden joists, the round-topped Norman arches and the later perpendicular architrave added on by Sir Hubert Harcombe when the abbey gifted the village of Rosebery Wood to the Lord of Trowchester in exchange for the eel-fishing rights on Peover Marsh.

Billy had a fund of historical information and local folklore to draw on, and usually managed to inform and entertain the tourists enough to earn a fiver or two in tips from each party. But today the bell ringers had been practising for an upcoming wedding and the walls had shaken with the clamour of harsh metallic voices, bellowing.

He'd had to shout his anecdotes until his head and throat hurt. People had shouted questions back at him, and he couldn't pick out the words from the bellowing of the bells.

He'd tried to keep it together, honestly he had. *Not hard enough.* But it . . . it shook him apart, all the noise. It got hooks into the fabric of him and teased and pulled all the threads until they began to unravel and unravel and fray and snap and . . .

The noise, the clamour, the discord, had shaken his tight grip open. The world had fallen out from his grasp because his skull was splitting and the noises were everywhere and everything was cracking and he couldn't fit it together again because it had shattered into too many shapes and there was no picture and there were no edge pieces and he couldn't make his fingers close on them anyway because his fingers had burst into too many shapes too.

So he'd locked the door behind the last curious couple and given them a perfunctory wave good-bye. Then he'd sat down.

He'd meant to sit down only for a moment, to use the peace for which he had been parched to refresh himself before he went home. But the thought of home was forbidding. When he felt this flayed, the mere living aura of his lodgers was like a cheese grater being drawn across his skin. Mrs. Webb's heavy presence above his head was saddening but tolerable. Mr. Kaminski, in the flat beneath his, was not. The man looked like a threat, sounded like a Russian mobster. His pressed suits talked of civilization, but there was something about his eyes that spoke of having seen men die, maybe of having killed them himself. Kaminski looked at Billy like the guns had looked at the rabbits, like a man looks at a small, nervous thing he intends to kill cleanly when the time comes.

Billy had taken a moment to nerve himself up to face that. And then . . . well. And then the black dog had come. It was sitting here with him, filling his mind with the fog of its breathing, sleeping heavy on his chest. So heavy.

He should get up. Something, something was happening today, he could almost put a name to it. Would, if his head was not so weighed down by the claws of the beast.

He didn't understand why he didn't get up when he knew he wanted to. He was a fundamentally wrong thing, a mistake, a freak of nature, and he was so tired. He was so tired of his miserable self, his miserable wretched self that *could not get up.*

But thinking of freaks stirred something to life in his head. What was it he was supposed to be doing today? Something flappy, black like a crow, spiralling to the ground on broken wings. What was . . .?

Creaking with the effort, like rusted train wheels grinding themselves loose, he thought, *It's Trowchester show tomorrow.*

Ten minutes later, when the sunlight had reached across the porch floor, groped up his body, and lain reassuring fingers on his cheeks, he added, *And it's tomorrow today.*

The words jogged something free. Wasn't he supposed to be at the meeting point in Werrington, all kitted up and with the sticks, at half past nine in the morning?

The warmth on his face lifted some of the mist inside him. He tilted his closed eyes up to it and opened like a sunflower.

Fuck yes. Yes, he was.

He checked his watch. It was eight fifteen. He had enough time. Just. If he ran to his house and changed his clothes, ate yesterday's toast for breakfast, strapped the sticks on his bike and pedalled like mad, he might make it yet.

First you've got to get up.

He let go of his knees. He put his feet down on the ground and slowly but surely he pushed himself upright until he was standing, cold as death and surprised as always to find out there was nothing physically wrong with him at all.

He took a stumbling step forward, his ankles almost turning under him, and it worked. His body answered his mind's commands again. He could walk.

Shoving all the darkness back into its place, he stamped on the lid of it until he could latch it down with the faulty catch—the world's least-entertaining jack put back into its box for the moment.

God, don't let them go without me! He took a deep, astonished breath, and started to run.

CHAPTER
THREE

An hour and a quarter later, Billy slammed on the brakes outside Werrington church hall just as the van was leaving the car park. He hurled himself off his bike and ran into the centre of the road, waving his arms. The minibus lurched to a halt with a grind of gears, and he saw Matt at the wheel, looking at him like a man who's just woken up and realised he's missing an arm.

While the minibus backed apologetically into a parking space, Billy locked his bike to a lamppost and unstrapped the stick bag from his carrier. His back tyre looked considerably worse for wear after carrying the weight of twelve long ash sticks and a further six short ones. Billy's legs weren't too happy about it either. Next time, one of the blokes with a car could bring the sticks.

"Sorry, Billy!" Parked again, Matt rolled the window down and hung a white-shirted elbow over it. "I thought you were on board already."

"No problem." Billy smiled through the residual panic, disappointed but not surprised that nobody had noticed he was missing. "Can someone—"

The doors at the back swung open, pushed by Graham and Pete. Billy passed them the sticks and clambered inside, over the dozen bags that cluttered the aisle and jingled when he nudged them with his feet. Nancy's drum in its carrying case stood like a small table in front of the only spare seat. Both seat and drum had been piled with ragged jackets, Colin's cameras, and the blacking kit.

"Are we all in now?" Matt called. "Okay, I'm going."

Billy had to hold on to the roof while they jogged and swayed over winter-pitted concrete, out of the car park and onto the smoother tarmac of the road. Then he dumped the jackets on the floor, resituated the blacking tin on his lap and eeled into the seat next to the other Billy.

"How do, Constant."

"How do, Billy-boy."

Billy-boy was a gentleman of seventy-five, with a beer belly and a beard that would have done Father Christmas proud. He had blacked up already, so his white moustache and eyebrows stood out startlingly from a face whose features could have been called handsome, fifty years ago. He passed Billy a battered hip flask with the top unscrewed, which Billy took hesitantly.

"That's last year's plums, Constant. You look like you need it. Up all night poaching, were you?"

"Something like that."

The side had solved the problem of having two Billies by the traditional means of nicknames. Naturally, the older of the two became "Billy-boy," or "the Boy" for short. Billy himself, since he had never yet missed a practice or a dance-out, had been christened "Constant Billy" after the dance of that name. This was often shortened to "Constant" to avoid confusion. He wasn't sure that there was really any confusion at work, but he liked the name and the praise that it implied.

The home-distilled plum brandy was hot and sharp on the tongue. It burnt his throat like paint stripper and settled uneasily in a stomach empty of anything but a slice of cold toast. Still, he took it for the kind gesture it was, and smiled. "It's not bad. Have you got a new still?"

"No, not at all. More like the old one's just getting settled. She's a bit of patina on her now. Stills're like people, aren't they—better when they've had a bit of time to mature." The Boy smiled and accepted Billy's hip flask in return. There was nothing special in it, just the same Famous Grouse whisky from the bottle he'd managed to eke out all year.

Traditionally, both flasks, having been opened, now had to be handed around to everyone in the side, and all other owners of flasks were obliged to join in the informal communion. So for a time, the minibus was full of hands rising out of seats, curving around seat backs to grope for the next bottle and pass it on. Seven men in the side meant seven flasks, seven sips of concentrated spirits, and it was only half past nine in the morning.

By virtue of their sex, the women of the side, in the four seats closest to the driver, could refuse to drink alcohol at any time without incurring the raised eyebrow of shame. They were having their own communion of coffee from a thermos, and declined the offer of early morning drunkenness in favour of talk about music and the birth of Nancy's first great-grandchild.

Fatigue and alcohol settled into a warm glow of peacefulness in Billy's chest, a bubble strong enough to hold back depression and darkness for a while at least. "How long until we get there?" he asked, wondering if he should black up in the van or wait until they arrived, when things might be a little more stable.

As he should have expected, this prompted a round of *I know the roads better than you do* one-upmanship from which he tentatively drew the conclusion that there were five different ways they could get to the Trowchester Summer Festival and that the timings could vary from an hour to an hour and a half. Once this had been properly chewed over, everyone had forgotten that Billy had asked the question at all. He was far too bored with the subject to ask again and risk setting it off a second time.

"Did we ever get a vote on Cotswold versus Border?" Matt called over his shoulder, prompting a general groan.

"I've just put the face paint on!"

"We've only brought the ragged jackets."

The Boy reached into his bag and triumphantly flourished a set of red baldrics. "I brought Cotswold kit. I could go for a bit of proper dancing instead of all this galumphing. There's no art in this Border stuff at all; it's just skipping about like big girls' blouses."

Billy sighed as the bagman's feathers began to flutter with wrath.

Graham, the bagman—the man in charge of the side's finances and bookings—was already fully dressed for the Border style of dancing. His face was so heavily matt black it looked like a hole beneath his top hat, which was festooned with crow feathers. Despite the heat from the risen sun warming the white metal roof, he sat like an angry blackbird in full plumage, tattered jacket closed to hide all evidence of a shirt. "I've said it a dozen times, Boy, the public don't want to watch Cotswold. They think it's silly. They like Border because it's masculine and aggressive and it looks pagan, and that's what's in at the moment."

Howls of protest burst from various corners of the bus, but Graham waded on like a lone voice of reason. "And big shows like this will pay us to do Border because it fits in with their . . ." he waved his hands in the air like windscreen wipers, describing vague shapes of indignation and scepticism ". . . theme—which seems to be a sort of 'Robin of Sherwood woowoo mystic ancient greenwood' sort of thing. So what they don't want is Cotswold with its ring of church bells and cricket and 'Is there honey still for tea?' fuddy-duddy wholesomeness."

At the continued cries of indignation, Graham's hands flew up, tossing a ball of helplessness into the air. "Don't look at me, I think it's as stupid as the rest of you do."

"I quite like Border," Annette put in. As the fiddler, she was theoretically entitled to leadership of the musicians, but she was locked in a polite war for the position with Margery, the melodeon player, whom nature had fitted out with a more dominant personality. "They have some very good tunes."

Cotswold versus Border was a conversation topic that could run and run. Everyone in the side had an opinion, and a strong one. Billy liked both, but that wasn't the point, of course. It was undeniably true that Cotswold required more technical expertise, was more of a challenge to dance, and was far less of a crowd pleaser.

Cotswold was also the real deal in terms of being the tradition that had been handed on intact from its fifteenth-century roots. The ethnologists of the nineteen hundreds had got there just in time to record the original Cotswold dances and tunes as they had been handed down for generations in each of the villages where they had been danced. By the time the erudite gentlemen had tried collecting the dances of the Welsh borders, the tradition had almost completely died out, with only a handful of original dances surviving. When revival fever blew through the borders, the majority of dances had had to be made up from scratch.

It irked Billy on a deep level that the public—having decided that Border *looked* more ancient, *looked* more pagan, and was therefore more exciting—had taken to the modern reconstruction with far more enthusiasm than they ever showed the real thing. It was surely wrong, on a moral level, to prefer the fake to the true. Yet people seemed happy to lie to themselves gleefully about the past, turning it into some kind of theme park and refusing to look at what was really there.

Billy hated it, hated playing along with it.

But, on the other hand, the Border styles were also fun and alive, changing with the times and vibrant with possibilities, an honest reflection of what the folk enjoyed *right now*, and he loved that. He also quite enjoyed the fact that the outfit scared the willies out of small children and gave the side an air of danger that Cotswold with its flowers and hankies, bless it, could never dream of.

Billy's opinion was complicated and would take a long time to explain. He supposed it was fortunate that no one ever left a gap in the conversation long enough for him to give it.

As if to mock their careful discussion of routes, the A23 was closed due to flooding, and the diversion choked with such heavy traffic the journey took an extra hour to complete. It was almost lunchtime when they pulled up in the exhibitors' car park at what looked like a very impressive affair indeed. Three finely shorn fields around the showground shimmered with multicoloured rows of vehicles. In the distance, a wire-mesh fence curved around several acres of enclosure. Feather-flags on carbon poles bent and strained at each gate. Inside, distant bouncy castles bulged like overweight rainbows. Billy could hear the cheery boom of someone talking over the PA in the central exhibition ring.

Spilling out of the sweaty hot minibus into the fresher warmth of the late-spring day, Billy wiped his brow on a spare towel and then waited as the musicians finished painting their faces. They had just begun to put the kit away when he plucked it out of Nancy's hands so he could do his own. *It's like I'm that character from* Ballad of Halo Jones, Billy thought. *If I don't remind people I'm here all the time, they forget I exist.*

A single strand of bells buckled on around his black trousers at the knee. He clipped his tankard to the black leather baldric he'd made for it and shrugged that over the shaggy jacket, covered in torn strips of cloth, that clipped around the throat and fell to mid thigh. Black silk top hat, somewhat worse for wear for being third-hand, with a pair of steampunk goggles with red lenses strapped to the front. Leather fingerless gloves and a long red-painted stick in his hand and he was ready to go.

The side stepped away from their van, and a change came over them. Before, they had been eleven not very remarkable people. Now, in kit and among the public, they were the strange and fearsome priests of a lost religion. Even the musicians—otherwise ordinary middle-aged women—clad all in black greatcoats, with faces as black as their coats under red-veiled, wide-brimmed black hats, were making festival-goers shiver with delighted terror at their eeriness as they passed.

When Billy walked through a crowd now, heads turned to follow him, eyes widened. He stood tall, let his stride open out, reflecting back confidence, arrogance, a little hint of danger in return for their wariness. His legs had more than recovered from this morning's bike ride. Warmth and company and half an hour's snooze had put some fire into him. He was ready to perform, to dance and laugh and heckle. To bask in the fact that, even though it only happened when he had a mask on, everyone was actually seeing him.

CHAPTER FOUR

"Look, I'm sorry. Maybe you can take it back?" Martin, now under his ninth-century name of Ametel, massaged the back of his head. The leather strap of his helmet had begun to rub through his arming cap. It felt like it was rubbing through his hair too, would leave him with a stripe of bald patch like a Celtic monk's tonsure. He wished the sun wasn't quite so warm. Light on chain mail looked very fine, but it made you feel like you were trapped in a toaster, and he didn't need this grief on top of everything else.

Stigand, who was new to reenactment, didn't know when to take a bit of friendly guidance. "That bloke on the Viking stall swore to me it was a Viking brooch. I'm a Viking, it's a Viking brooch, what's the problem?"

Martin cast a *help me!* look towards his second-in-command, Rolf. Got a sympathetic eye roll in return but nothing more, and wasn't it great that Martin had to handle *everything* himself? Surely there was someone in the society better equipped than him to argue authenticity? Some backup somewhere would have been nice.

At least Rolf was dressed for the part, his spangenhelm hand welded and worn through a ten-year career with *that other society we don't name*, until the cheek pieces were impregnated with genuine dirt and sweat, and the shine of the metal glinted unevenly over dozens of dents.

His armour was much the same. Top-quality chain mail of riveted rings, over a gambeson of leather that had once been woad dyed but was now so stained with ground-in fat that the colour of it couldn't be guessed. Rolf was such a fiend for authenticity he stored his chain mail in pig fat to simulate the pigs' stomachs in which it was said the Vikings sewed their armour to keep it gleaming and waterproof for long voyages. Certainly the smell of him was something you rarely encountered in modern life.

The new recruits were a different matter. Martin couldn't fault the kit of Kayleigh (also known as Ulf). Basic, but entirely in line with the guides, and she'd even managed to make her own turn shoes. The colours were excellent—bright weld yellow and undyed sheep's-wool brown. The weave was perfect in the cloth, thread count per inch was fine. She'd even overstitched the seams with a contrasting undyed sheep's-wool white, in a display of dedication to which some of his old members hadn't yet risen.

But that chest! Double D at least, and obvious as a neon sign. Plus, she'd pulled her hair up in a high ponytail, like Sif from the Thor films, and done her face in eyeliner and lip gloss.

He sighed. "Ulf, you've got to make an effort to look less like a woman. Firstly the makeup's right out. Secondly, ponytail gathered at the base of the neck, or put it under a hat. Thirdly, can someone lend her a gambeson? You might want to cover that . . ." He gestured somewhat helplessly towards her front. "You've got to disguise your shape. The rule is, women are allowed on the battlefield so long as they look like men. A sports bra might help. Squash it all a bit, you know?"

Stigand sniggered, and Kayleigh swiped at him with her borrowed shield. "At least I haven't bought a bit of overpriced jubbly tat. It's so gay! I told you."

"It is not gay!"

Martin scratched at the sore stripe in his hair again and hoped he had not visibly flinched. He should *say* something. Something along the lines of, *If you don't like gay, you'd better get out of my society.* But God it was hard enough being one minority. He really wasn't sure he could face being two.

Besides, Bretwalda needed the new members, needed to grow, needed not to have people worried about watching their language, or worse, pissing off because they couldn't bear to have a leader who was both black and gay.

He was being a coward, he knew that, but there was too much to do, too much to worry about right now. This could wait. "Stigand. It *is* jubbly."

The brooch in question, well, he could barely bring himself to look at it, the experience was so painful. An electroplated Thor's hammer that owed more to Marvel than to mythology, covered in enamelled designs and studded with semiprecious jewels that glittered in the sunlight.

"I can't count the number of ways that this is wrong." He turned it over. "Look at this clasp—invented in the 1980s. Pseudo-Celtic knotwork. Even if the Vikings weren't an entirely different people to the Celts, with an entirely different style of art, the Celts themselves would piss on this as making no sense. Viking jewellers didn't use any of these stones, and in any case, they certainly hadn't invented faceting yet. You try and wear this, I will ban you from the field."

It had already been a very long, very hard day, after a very long, very hard night.

Angry with the Head and everything she represented, Martin had taken up McKay's offer to teach his class yesterday afternoon. He had gone home seething and packed his car. He had driven here, seething. He had put up his own heavy Viking ship-tent, assembled the firebox, and filled it with sand. Assembled his bed frame and made up a bed with a blow-up mattress and reindeer-skin rugs. He had put out the benches and the cauldrons, the tripod, the trivet, the baskets of spare mugs and plates.

Then he'd cut up some wood, started a fire, fetched water from the standpipe, boiled a kettle, and made himself another Pot Noodle, which he ate in solitary splendour before retiring to bed at midnight. At which time—naturally—the other senior members of the garrison had arrived, shining their headlights through the walls and shouting as they put up their own tents.

This morning he had risen at dawn. The sunlight through the white canvas of the tent left little option. Besides, some unutterable bastard over in the World War II encampment kept blowing reveille on a bugle, and at five o'clock in the morning the sound carried like an air-raid warning.

So the day had started with first-day-of-a-show-lack-of-sleep dizziness. Things improved a little over breakfast, once he had cut more wood, remade the fire from the embers, fetched more water, boiled another kettle for three black coffees, and then eaten a plateful of bacon and eggs.

By the time he'd got dressed in kit—a story behind every piece of clothing, every one made by himself or a friend, and precious in a way nothing of disposable modern-day life was valuable—he'd come out of his tent and had one of those *it must have been just like this* moments.

Athelstan and his family had set up their weaving enclosure by then, and Edith, in charge of the society's encampment, had managed to erect shady pavilions under which the warriors could lie in the heat of the day. She'd dressed the canvas rooms with food and artefacts of the period and was now feeding the picketed horses their hay.

For just one moment, so long as he didn't lift his eyes above the rope barrier that cut off their encampment from the rest of the show, he might have been waking in the ninth century. Everything he saw was Viking or Saxon, handmade, perfect for its purpose, simple, beautiful, and right.

The early morning air had smelled of woodsmoke, dew, and horses. Edith already in full kit—mantle and kirtles and wimple—was like a figure from an illuminated manuscript brought to life.

His troubles had been struck dumb, and he'd thought, *It's going to be okay.*

Then Edith had come over to ask for money for the garrison's food, handing him a stack of forms listing who had come, whether they were paying for a full day's food or just lunch, how many children were present for whom she could only claim half a ration, and the moment had been lost. It had been one long administrative niggle from then until now.

Meanwhile, Stigand was still refusing to back down. "You've got orange stones in your necklace, so why can't I—"

"I have got carnelian beads because my character is from the kingdom of Meroe in Nubia, one of whose principle exports was carnelian. Unless you also happen to have a Sudanese parent, that excuse isn't going to fly for you."

"But the bloke said!"

"Stigand. Are you going to believe the word of some shopkeeper who makes a living selling horned helmets and 'genuine Viking claymores' to people who don't give a toss whether that's what they were really like, or are you going to believe your authenticity officer, who reads archaeological journals for a hobby? Hint. One will get you onto the battlefield and one will not."

"What am I supposed to do about it, then?"

Martin took his watch out of his belt pouch. There was just about time to bolt down some lunch before they had to go on and wow the public with their martial prowess. He sighed again. "Go back to the stall where you got it and ask for a refund. You were wearing kit when you bought it, right?"

Stigand nodded, his head still bent regretfully over the abomination of a brooch.

"Well, if he told you that was a Viking brooch, he told you a load of bollocks. He was trying it on because we're a new society and he thinks we don't know the score. Tell him if you don't get a refund, I'll send Rolf down to have a word with him. We may be a new society, but he knows all our *thegns* from way back, and he needs reminding that he can't slip shit like that past us. All right?"

The newbie still looked surly and unconvinced. Martin wondered if this was one recruit who would not come back after his first show. Thought it would be like a live action *World of Warcraft*, did he? Thought he'd get to be oh so cool, because it was just a game and who gave a fuck, right? If that was the case, if the guy didn't care about history enough to want to do it properly, Martin didn't need him anyway.

"Go on. Do it now, before you miss lunch. We're on in three-quarters of an hour."

The rest of the muster of warriors fortunately turned up nothing to complain about. Like Rolf and Martin himself, these were all ex-members of *that other society*.

While fully in agreement with its ethos of being the most accurate depiction of life in the Dark Ages that was to be found in the country, they'd split from *that society* for purely personal reasons. The usual stories: political infighting, cliques, personality clashes. The tendency of Martin's old group leader to spend the night around the fire telling homophobic jokes and needling him for having no sense of humour when he didn't laugh. Even the fact that Martin ended up as a perpetual chew toy between people who wanted to put him into photos of the society for PC reasons, and people who wanted him kept out of the photos because he wasn't what the public wanted to see when they looked for Vikings.

Bretwalda was meant to be Martin's refuge, a society with the same high standards, but without the pissing contests. Maybe even a place where he could dare, one day, to openly bring a boyfriend without the certainty that he'd be the subject of every dirty joke around the campfire for years.

He just hadn't really expected it to come with this much grief. Now even Rolf was looking at him askance. "If he comes back as surly as he was when he went, I'm not sure I want him on the field in charge of a spear."

They had grown a great deal since Martin formed the society two months ago, with a round robin letter to his friends in *that other society*. There was a sense of hope over the whole encampment—the hope that this time they could all do their thing without petty little power plays getting in the way. But it still only amounted to a grand total of twenty warriors. With an audience like this, they couldn't afford to lose even one. He really didn't want Bretwalda's first big show to be an embarrassment to everyone.

"Put him on the field," he said now. "All that adoration will give him the motivation to want to do it right in future."

"And if he puts someone's eye out?"

Martin shrugged, pretty sure that even Kayleigh was good enough to prevent that happening. Truth was, she had the makings of a good line commander. "Bit of gore? The crowd'll love it."

Speak of the devil, he thought, coming in under the work shelter to saw at a loaf of bread with his handseax. Someone had loaned Kayleigh a padded gambeson which disguised her figure, and a helmet which disguised her hair. Her face was washed clean of makeup, and she had even given herself a five-o'clock shadow with some ash from the fire. He was impressed and ready to say so, but her expression was easily as sullen as Stigand's.

"She says—" Kayleigh gestured dismissively at Edith "—I have to help her with the cooking. Why do I have to help her with the cooking just cos I'm a girl? I don't do cooking in real life, and I don't mean to start now."

Privately, Martin thought she had a point. In *that other society* there had been no rule that the women had to cook, but still they had somehow ended up doing it anyway. He wasn't sure if they preferred it, or if they just stepped in because no one else could be bothered. That was something at least he could improve on.

"Everyone should get to do everything," he said, and his teacherly side prompted him to add, "I'll draw up a rota after the battle."

He folded roughly chopped ham, raw onions, and cheese into his wedge of bread. It had been a hard day, he thought again as he washed down the sandwich with a leather mug full of apple juice, and watched as the warriors began to muster into a two-column marching formation behind Biscop Weyland's cross. A hard day, and it was still only half over. But when they blew the harsh discordant notes of the great hunting horns and all the milling public turned to look at his small army with admiration, he still thought it was a good one.

Let it be a good battle, with single combats between some of the seasoned warriors who know how to put on a good show, with some drama and some good death scenes and no actual injuries. Let us impress the organisers so we get asked back. Let us thrill the crowds and make more starry-eyed youngsters want to join up. And let us have fun, so all our newbies come out of the ring floating on their own glory, reassured that it may take extra effort to do it well, but we are fucking good, and it's worth it.

CHAPTER
FIVE

With less than a minute to go, the Stomping Griffins drew up outside the central arena and offloaded a dozen bags onto the hay bales that both defined the area and served as seats for the inner ring of audience. Here by the entrance stood a stand for the announcer, a tall scaffolding pole with loudspeakers attached to the top of it. The microphone itself was out in the centre of the ring, in the hand of a woman who was just winding up a display of falconry.

They could vividly hear the bull-roarer vibration along the string of her lure as she twirled it in the air. "Ah, and there he comes. Over by the helter-skelter. Keep your eyes on that dot."

Billy did, and saw it unfold into a spectacular tawny-winged bird with psychopath eyes. It swooped straight at the rat on a string, looking leisurely until the final blinding rush, caught the meat in big yellow claws, and allowed itself to be drawn down to sit on the woman's heavy glove, shrugging as if cynically unimpressed by the clapping of the crowd.

"That concludes the falconry demonstration."

The announcer walked out to relieve the falconer of the microphone. Switching it off, he brought it back with him to go into a huddle with the Stomping Griffins' musicians.

"No one's going to hear you if you're not amplified out there. So where would you like me to hold the mic? Somewhere in the centre, around here?"

"I think, if you stood by Christine," Annette was saying, "at the other end from Nancy. If we put the pennywhistle at one extreme and the drum at the other, you could hold the mic closer to the quietest instrument. What are we starting with, boys?"

Matt offered the announcer a distracted smile. "We'll start with a dance called 'Blue-Eyed Stranger.' Then I'll shout them out as we go along."

A glissade of bells sounded out as the side moved into a six-man formation. That was when Billy first noticed the horns and the chanting. Noise crashed at them from everywhere of course. Steam fairground organs played Mozart. A stall selling little statuettes of dragons curled around highly coloured glass gems was belting out "All Around My Hat" by Steeleye Span. Children were shrieking while their parents yelled. Billy had tried, as he always had to try, to tune it all out, so it had been easy to overlook the additional sound of approaching footsteps and the jangle of horses' tack.

But then a guy who looked like he ought to be sacking churches and setting innocent monks on fire took the mic right out of the announcer's hand.

"What the . . . ?"

Almost as one, the side turned in bewilderment. Billy found a small army of Vikings bearing down on him, preceded by a purple-clad priest with a nasty-looking mace at his belt. Unhesitatingly, the priest walked out into the arena, carrying a polished processional cross with a banner beneath it.

The heavies went to follow. A guy in a helmet with odd, owl-like frames of metal around his eyes. One with an axe as tall as he was and a shield Billy associated with the Normans. A third, a startlingly and unexpectedly black Viking wearing a necklace of white shells and carnelian over his hauberk. All of them built like human tanks and ironclad in armour that hung far too heavy, and stank far too rankly, to be just for show.

Those swords were convincing—not flash enough, not decorated enough, not spiky enough to have been made up by some modern dreamer. A part of Billy recognised and respected the fact that these guys looked like they meant business. Another part was too busy going, *What the fuck? You don't get to ignore me too. This is* our *spot! Our time. Get out of it!*

He wasn't the only one enraged. Sometimes, when the side danced on a public road, some tosser of a driver who thought he didn't have time to wait out a single dance would attempt to drive his car straight through the set, expecting dancers and musicians to move aside for him. It never happened that way. The side closed in. The dancers would be deliberately obstructive. The musicians would stand, unmoving, until the car's bumper touched their knees—and if it got that far, the driver would find himself surrounded by angry protective men with sticks. So there was no way—*no way*—the side was going to meekly let a bunch of weirdos in dress-up push past them.

To a person, Billy and his side closed around the gap into the arena, orphaning the "priest" who now stood in the centre of the ring. Matt turned on the organiser. "It does say the Stomping Griffins are on now, doesn't it?"

The poor man took off his flatcap and smoothed down his bald patch contemplatively. "It does..."

"Right, so—"

"But it also says, 'Combat display by Bretwalda.' Sorry, we've double booked for some reason. Maybe you can—"

"Well, we were obviously here first." Matt signalled to the musicians. Nancy had placed her enormous drum on the ground, a gorgeous red-painted thing with the team's black griffin on the side, its goat-skin drumheads tensioned with snow-white ropes. Now she picked it up and shrugged on the harness.

She hit it. *Boom*! And again. *Boom*! The melodeon struck up with a bagpipe-like drone just as one of the Vikings on horseback was trying to shoulder his way through the close-packed black of the dancers. Maybe the drumbeat spooked it. Maybe it was the way the Boy gave an automatic leap in answer to the music. Perhaps it didn't like this big, dark, faceless flapping thing jumping at its nose. All Billy knew was that the horse kicked out, its hoof punching a hole in the drum. Wood splintered and the horse bucked and danced to try to shake this terrifying red thing off its leg.

Bravely but very unwisely, Nancy tried to pull her ruined drum away. Billy saw the disaster coming but not fast enough to stop it. He was still running forward when the full weight of the horse drove up against the eighty-year-old's shoulder, picked her off the ground and threw her. She went sailing in a way that might have been comical in a woman a quarter of her age, slammed the edge of her back into the straw bales, and rolled over them to lie still on the inner edge of the arena.

"You fucker!" Billy had a stick in his hand. He didn't think twice about running up to the horseman and belting him across the armoured thigh for being a sick fucker who rode down old ladies. "What do you think you're doing, you fucking wanker?!"

The rest of the side were with him in a kind of synergy that only ever happened in the dancing when they were really on form. Pudgy Matt and the Boy—who was only five years younger than Nancy himself—the normally straitlaced Pete, terminally sceptical Colin, and suave Andy just as fired up by his side. Margery had seized a spare stick and was wading in too, while Annette and Christine were on either side of Nancy's fallen form, carefully proffering hankies and support.

The horseman didn't even have the decency to reply, instead leaning down over his mount's neck and whispering to it. But the rest of the army poured out from all around the animal and closed ranks in front of it.

"Fucking watch what you're doing with the fucking horse!" Spectacles-helm guy got up in Billy's face and pushed him in the chest. A hell of a lot of weight there. The shove knocked Billy off his feet, but dancing had made him agile enough to twist in the air and come down foursquare and balanced.

"Did you see what he did? Did you see him knock down an old lady?"

"She fucking asked for it."

Even the hard-nosed spectacles-Viking himself seemed to realise he had stepped over a line with that. His eyes went wide, and he backpedalled a little, raising his hands. But it was far too late.

"You utter . . .!" Graham danced on a Wednesday night, and did karate on a Friday. A tall athletic man, with whom Billy was in competition for the unspoken acknowledgement of being the side's best dancer, he wore a short-trimmed red beard and would have looked quite at home in armour, if the roles were reversed. Billy's untutored slice to the leg had bounced off the horseman's chain mail and been disregarded, but when Graham hit spectacles-guy in the sternum with the heel of his open hand, the guy reeled back five paces and went down.

Billy heard the whisper-snick sounds of swords being drawn—long blade-shapes of steel sliding against the metal-lined mouths of scabbards. He could see they were blunt, the points carefully rounded, the edges a good millimetre thick and smoothed off so as not to break the skin. But they were still heavy steel bars a good two feet long. They might not cut but, like the side's sticks, he was pretty sure they could break bones.

Some of his righteous anger faltered. There were rules to this—the other side backed down in front of the threat. If they had any decency, they backed down and did not force actual blows. But this lot weren't conceding anything. Even the ragged edges of the army, thin guys and short androgyns with nothing more menacing to their name than long tunics and itchy trousers, were massing in support of their leaders. Behind the swords, the jackals of this army were aiming spears at the side.

In the long, tense moment that followed, the black Viking caught Billy's eye. He could see his own thoughts reflected on the man's handsome face. *This is all getting a little out of hand.*

"Guys," Billy said, tentatively. "Do we really want to go there?" Right was on their side, overwhelmingly, but he didn't want to end up with a conviction for affray. He didn't want the Griffins to get a reputation as a bunch of bully boys it wasn't safe to ask to your event. He didn't want this to get to a point where someone would have to get the police involved.

And that was, of course, when the police arrived. Two constables in high-vis vests, striding along behind the organiser, whom Billy hadn't even noticed leaving.

The woman PC pushed herself between Graham and Norman-shield-guy. A little thing, half their height, she had dyed-auburn hair growing out black, tied back fiercely from a face that said it wasn't at all impressed. "All right, lads, calm down. Back off a pace, both of you."

Thank God for the voice of authority, Billy thought, and did as she asked, turning round to check on Nancy. The sight of her sitting unaided on a straw bale, cradling a paper cup of tea in both hands and smiling, brought him further down from his desire to smite the evildoers. It brought further into his mind the thought of what this whole incident must look like to outsiders—the sort of outsiders who were thronging the ring two deep and standing on the seats to get a better view.

Oh shit.

"'Scuse me. Just step aside there please . . ." The organiser shepherded a man with a fishing rod through the awkwardly milling combatants and sent him into the arena to tell the "priest" to come back in. "And now, ladies and gentlemen, in a change to our published programme, the fly fishing demonstration has been brought forward from three o'clock. That's the fly fishing demonstration now, and we'll keep you posted on what's coming next when we have it sorted out."

"I think you'd all better come with me." The WPC's partner, a Sikh with the black-and-white chequered band and badge of the police tied around his sharply folded turban, had Graham and spectacles-helm-guy by the elbows, propelling them firmly and inexorably away from the ring.

Billy peeled out of the mass of dancers to offer Nancy his arm. She smiled at him, but didn't take it, rising under her own steam and straightening up with the pride and stubborn resilience of the Blitz generation. She still looked like a vengeful goddess, more so with her hat knocked off and her long white hair come loose from its bun. Like the Morrigan, or the Crone—an aspect of womanhood long past putting up with the foolishness of others.

"Don't fuss," she said, walking stiffly in a black clot of Griffins behind the Viking army's spear-fodder. Annette came at the very rear, carrying the corpse of the beautiful drum.

CHAPTER SIX

The police guided them to a secluded spot: a strip of bare grass between the back of the crepe van and the wire fence. Martin had time to think as they walked, time to get a good look at the woman who'd been thrown by Jasper, and realise that when the weirdos in black yelled about her being an old lady, they were speaking nothing but the truth.

It was hard to tell what any of them were under that thick layer of pitch-black face paint—and he had to admit the black faces had set him against them from the start. But now he looked closer, it was possible to see the woman really was someone's granny. He was appalled to think she could have broken a hip, broken her back, and all because no one had the sense to talk about who went on first.

"Listen," he said as soon as they arrived and the WPC had brought out her notebook. "I take responsibility."

"Oh yes, why's that, sir?"

"I'm the leader of Bretwalda. I should have intervened earlier. I shouldn't have even let it get started. I don't quite know why it did."

"They spooked Jasper." Snorri had dismounted, but stood with his hand reassuringly on his horse's shoulder. Jasper too had calmed down and was grazing on the nettles which grew high around the fence, though his back hooves stomped from time to time with lingering nerves. Snorri seemed torn between an animal lover's indignation that anyone could blame his charge for anything, and an understandable guilt over the possible injury of a very old lady.

One of the crow-people—Martin gathered they were morris dancers, but they weren't anything like what he pictured when he thought of the term—had brought a plastic chair from outside the crepe van for their casualty. She sat in it looking very composed and severe while a fluttery woman with a pennywhistle between her teeth redid her bun with numerous hairpins.

"We wouldn't have spooked the horse if you hadn't been trying to barge in." That was the plump guy who seemed to be their leader. Schoolteachery, Martin thought, as one who should know. One of those men who came into teaching with unreasonably high ideals, and grew more and more disheartened with every year as the world around him failed to live up to them.

"That's probably true," Martin acknowledged to the police. "We were booked in the arena at one thirty. We were very keen to get on. We're a new society and it's our first show, and it would make a lot of difference to our long-term financial viability if we were asked back here next year. We wanted to be on time."

The WPC made a note. Her partner's stance relaxed from battle ready to at ease. Martin spared his father a grudging moment of acknowledgement. On settling in Britain, his father had taken elocution lessons to learn to speak with Received Pronunciation, replacing his Sudanese accent with the British accent that meant power, education, and wealth. He had married a woman with the same accent and passed it along to his children, drumming into them the necessity of sounding like one of the elite. And Martin had to admit that people did indeed take him more seriously once he spoke, as if he'd given them the Masonic handshake. Perhaps that was why his father was also so anti-gay. He was anti anything that might put himself or his children on society's—heh—blacklist. He'd be absolutely livid if he ever found out Martin had risked attracting the attention of the police. Another thing to keep quiet about.

Please, he thought, *please let me get out of this without an arrest.*

"Plus, there's a certain image you've got to keep up if the public is going to accept you as fearsome warriors," Martin went on, deliberately earnest, as posh as he could be. "You can't visibly stop for a chitchat before walking on. We'd confirmed earlier that that was our spot, so we thought they were just being difficult, not letting us through."

He shrugged, shamefaced, as he looked at their victim, the wreck of what must have been a very well-loved instrument, and all the court of worried people standing around her. People who had every right to be pissed off. "We did barge in. We didn't think that's what we were doing, but we did."

Now he was able to see them all closer, Martin's attention was caught by the tall bloke who stood behind the old lady as though he were a bodyguard behind the throne of a queen.

They all wore the same thing, these guys: black boots, black trousers with bells on a strip of red leather tied just beneath their knees. A huge coat covered all over with dangling strips of black cloth that rose and fell as they moved, giving the appearance of feathers. On the back of the coats, red tatters replaced black over their shoulders and down their spines, like a Tiw rune, or perhaps like bloody wings.

Their blackened faces were shadowed under black top hats, some with black feathers, some with red bird skulls. Martin had to hand it to them. It was an eerie look. As someone who knew something about dressing to scare the shit out of an enemy, he was begrudgingly impressed.

But it made it difficult to regard them as people rather than as some sort of raven priesthood. And that made the man with the goggles on his hat stand out all the more. Martin wasn't sure he forgave them the blackface, but oh, lord, it made that bloke's blue eyes stand out as startling and as luminous as the eyes of a Siamese cat. Beautiful. He couldn't stop looking.

It was honestly hard to see their faces, the paint reflecting no light at all, and so all he got apart from those eyes was a sense of stature. The guy had to be six feet tall, and built like a runner, sinewy and slender. Something about his poise kept dragging Martin's gaze back to him, even when he closed his startling eyes. He had the air of one of Tolkien's dark elves, a beautiful and mysterious creature capable of walking unseen among lesser mortals.

And that was just plain ludicrous. Martin didn't know what he was thinking, concentrating on long, long legs in tight black trousers, and not on imminent disaster. He should rein in his hormones and get back behind his fledgeling society. Figure out how best to handle this without turning it into a disaster from which they would never recover.

"I'm sorry, ma'am." He addressed the old lady personally, coming out from the shelter of his companions, deliberately crossing the distance to meet one to one, instead of as part of a crowd. "Jasper's generally a pretty placid horse, or we wouldn't take him out on the battlefield. I think he'd just never seen anything like you lot before. You're pretty scary looking."

"I suppose we are," she agreed, graciously. "I can see how he might have been spooked. I don't blame him. I shouldn't have tried to . . ." She cast a regretful look at her drum, and he understood that she valued it as he valued his sword—that it too was a thing removed from modern, disposable, commercial life.

"I will of course pay for the drum to be repaired. Or if that can't be done, then I'll pay for a new one. We have insurance that will cover it."

That brought a softening throughout the morris troop. The old lady even smiled—sad but genuine. "Thank you. I wonder if it could be repaired? It was my husband's, for years and years before he died, and I was hoping to leave it to the side when I went to join him."

"I'm just glad . . ." It felt worse and worse, the more he got to think of these people as people. It took all the gloss of tribal conflict off the altercation and left it a silly spat between civilised grown-ups who ought to have known better. "I'm just glad that was the only harm done. I'd never have forgiven myself if you'd been hurt."

The blue eyes behind her shoulder changed shape. Smiling, maybe. Martin smiled in return. Damn it, he had to somehow get that guy to wash the paint off. He itched to see his face for real.

Even though he's a racist arsehole? Even though they all are?
You don't know that.
Yeah right.

Because there was always the possibility that this lot were part of the *little England, everything was better in the days of yore before all these bloody immigrants* strain of folk dancers, and nothing yet had said otherwise.

"So . . ." The WPC referred to her notebook for the name. "Mrs. Cleveland. I have sufficient evidence to support an arrest on charges of affray, or even ABH. Do you intend to press charges?"

"I don't think so. I rather think it was a misunderstanding. And I don't think I am actually bodily harmed, so that one wouldn't stick. I suggest we just shake on it and call it a day."

This time, when Martin stole another glance at the young man's blue eyes, he found them looking back. Hard to read as they were, without the small clues of the rest of the face, he thought they were warm and puzzled and curious. A gaze that made him want to smile and preen a little, with his skin prickling and a flutter of interest low in his belly.

"And Mr. Cartersly." This time the WPC addressed Rolf, who was still rubbing his breastbone, where the redheaded dancer had broken out with his unexpected kung fu. "Do you intend to press charges against Mr. Patterson?"

Rolf took off his helmet. Since he all but lived in it, this was a momentous occasion, like Judge Dredd doing the same. There was a reason for this—his buzz cut of dark stubble was only suitable for a slave in the ninth century—but it still made being able to see his whole face seem disconcertingly intimate.

He grinned. "Are you kidding? That was some punch. You at all interested in joining us, mate? Because I've got a spot in the left flank of the army that would be perfect for you."

Having left the ring in the sure hands of the fly fisherman, the fete organiser stepped out from beyond the Portaloos, with a harried expression and a clipboard clutched to his chest.

"Things seem to have calmed down here," the policeman told him. "Do you wish to make an official complaint?"

"I wish . . ." The organiser's flatcap had come off entirely now. He was using it as a stressball, twisted and clutched in one hand. "I wish stuff like this didn't happen *all the time*. But you know it does. And I haven't got the time or energy to sue them all. If they're sorted out and ready to go on, I'm happy to fit them back into the programme in the last two slots of the afternoon."

"All right, then." The policeman nodded to the WPC, who made a final note. "You'll be happy to know I'm not going to make any arrests at this time. But WPC Harker and I are going to be at this fete all weekend, and we will have an eye on all of you. Any more funny business and that decision can be rescinded. Are we clear?"

A general mumble of agreement from everyone. Martin shook hands with plump-crow-guy and was pleasantly surprised when the grip turned out to be no more than firm and friendly. He'd been expecting a competitive vice.

"Listen," he said, partly out of the giddy elation of not being arrested, partly out of the desire not to let the blue-eyed stranger get away. "It looks like neither of us is on for another three hours. Why don't you all come back to our encampment? We've got benches and a fire. We can brew up tea and coffee for all, and I'll go get everyone chips."

He didn't miss the way they all turned to Mrs. Cleveland for her decision, but he thought it was understandable enough. She glanced at Martin, undecided, and over her shoulder, like a bright-eyed shadow, the lithe young man looked at him too.

"You'd be doing me a favour, honestly. I feel kind of terrible about all this."

That was true. Whether or not he continued to feel terrible would depend on what they did now. A self-righteous and angry rejection, and Martin could rule them all off as a bunch of probably racist, BNP-supporting wankers and stop feeling quite so guilty. And if they accepted the hand of friendship and came, he could also stop feeling guilty, and start feeling positively intrigued.

"That would be very nice," she said and stood up, prepared to set off right now. "And you can tell me all about what it is that you do. That chain mail looks terribly heavy, for example. Is it as bad as it looks?"

Martin grinned. Now here was a topic he could talk about all day long. "It weighs approximately three stone, on its own. With the helmet, sword, scramaseax, and shield, I'm carrying about five stone in equipment. When you take it off at the end of the day, it feels like you're floating."

Both horses had already left, being taken back to their makeshift paddock. Rolf ushered the rest of the army away, looking back to Martin as he did so. Martin smiled again. "If you go with Rolf, he'll show you around. Chips for everyone? Salt and vinegar?"

He collected the orders. Didn't like the beanpole's snooty look, but the rest of them seemed decent enough. The young man he'd been eyeing had disappeared, and Martin had a flash of thinking maybe he really was some otherworldly spirit in disguise, before he reappeared from behind the crepe van where he'd been returning the chair.

Ha! Martin thought gleefully. *Separated from the pack.* He moved in, warily elated like a hunter closing on his prey. "Hey."

Oh, the way the guy moved. Like . . . appropriately enough, like a dancer, all assurance and grace. His half-obscured expression belied it though, caught off-balance as though he didn't know what to do about being singled out for conversation by a black guy. Martin's heart sank a little.

"Hey?"

"I don't think I can carry enough chips for thirty people on my own. Any chance of a hand?"

A duck of the head to try to conceal a quick and secret smile, and Martin thought, *Or maybe he's just shy,* and was ridiculously charmed from head to foot.

"Yes, of course." The smile grew, although the blue eyes were now focussed somewhere to one side of Martin's waist, the guy's head tilted away. Martin struggled with the desire to take the man's face by his sooty chin and turn it so that he could not carry on avoiding Martin's admiration. Just as he had dismissed this as too intrusive for a first meeting, the dancer laughed at himself and straightened up.

He grazed Martin's gaze with his own for one blue-hot moment. "I'm sorry. I'm just not used to people talking to me. To be honest, I'm not even used to them seeing me at all. I'm Billy, by the way. Billy Wright."

Martin took his hand and blessed whoever had invented handshakes. Long fingers, rough from some kind of manual work, sinewy and strong. Pulse beating in Martin's palm like a drumbeat.

"Martin Deng. And I haven't been able to stop looking at you since all this started."

CHAPTER
SEVEN

The chip van had been disguised as a pavilion reminiscent of Robin Hood. Inside it, the cooks all wore the narrow green hats with long feathers of the Disney movie.

As they joined the queue, Martin took his helmet off and hung it in the crook of his arm by the strap, like a particularly butch lady's handbag. His long hair, in a curtain of braids, was tied back with a woven band, the authenticity not even slipping enough for elastic. His face looked less harsh without the framework of metal, but his expression was troubled.

As Billy wondered if Martin's earlier comment had been flirtation or criticism, Martin sighed, seeming to brace himself up for an unavoidable confrontation. "Look, I've got to ask you this. You do know how offensive the blackface is, don't you? Are you meaning to be racist or are you just doing it by accident?"

Billy took a step back, accidentally jostling a large woman with terrible sunburn who was waiting in the queue behind him. His heart sank dangerously low in the bubble of his current mental-okayness, distending the sides of it, threatening to make it pop.

Another one of these complicated questions and no one else from the side there to dismiss it in a sound bite. Everyone got fed up with Billy's explanations. Everyone seemed to think he was incapable of getting to the point. No one seemed willing to keep listening long enough to realise that he had several different points at once.

"It's . . . difficult," he tried, and then despised himself for wishing the question hadn't come up. Martin wasn't asking out of intellectual curiosity like most of the people who raised this issue. He was asking because he wanted to know—depending on the answer—whether his feelings mattered to Billy. Whether Billy thought he was a real person or not. "Complicated."

Martin's thoughtful expression slipped into a minor register, but he didn't push or dismiss Billy, yet. He just nodded at the queue ahead of them. "We'll be here for half an hour. You've got plenty of time to explain 'complicated.'"

"Seriously?" Billy was astonished. Since when had anyone ever given him the chance to give his opinion with all the nuances? Martin would doubtless interrupt and ride all over the explanation halfway through, but the offer in itself was unprecedented. "Okay, then."

He took off his hat and used it to fan his hot face as he tried to marshal his thoughts. "Well, the blacking comes from Victorian times, when morris dancing had been made illegal. Um, the Victorians thought of it as aggressive begging and decided they were going to stamp it out."

"Heh." Martin cradled his helmet in one hand as tenderly as if it were a nest full of baby birds. "They're responsible for the idea that Viking helmets had horns, you know. Tossers. We're never going to see the back of that one."

Billy laughed, relieved that things were friendly between them, his fragile normality still holding up.

"To be fair, they had a point about the dancing." He waved a hand at his get up. "In the Border and Molly traditions, the dancers were generally agricultural workers. By the end of the winter, money and food would be thin on the ground, so they'd go round the more affluent houses and dance. Normally, people would put some money in the hat, or hand out beer and food, and everyone would be happy and no one would get hurt."

Up by the hatch of the chip van, a live role playing mage with a very fine dragon puppet on her arm was reaching for a battered sausage with onion rings. She added salt and vinegar to her chips and then came past them both, offering them the special weirdos-of-the-world-unite nod of recognition. The minidragon nipped one of Billy's tatters in its jaws as she passed, startling a laugh out of him.

They edged further up the queue.

"But?"

"But sometimes the house owners would be the kind that didn't want to give their hard-earned money to a group of burly strangers at the door, and they'd tell them, 'Be off with you, you disgraceful beggars, and get a real job.'"

Still Billy hadn't quite got to the point, and still Martin was patiently waiting for him, neither pushing nor changing the subject. Billy felt . . . too much. Seen, heard . . . exposed. He was unused to it, and it felt frighteningly intimate.

"If that happened, the dancers would do something to show their displeasure. Usually they were plough boys, so they'd come back to that house in the middle of the night and plough up stripes in all their careful lawns. But because there was that threat there, it meant that the dancers could be accused of demanding money with menaces. It meant that the householders could set the police on them and have them arrested."

Billy arrived at his point, finally. "So the morris dancers got into the habit of going dancing in disguise. All year round, they'd had strips of cloth sewn inside their jackets for extra warmth, but now they turned their coats inside out, so they couldn't be recognised by their clothes. And they rubbed soot all over their faces, so no one could recognise those either."

He laughed, nervously. "I didn't really believe it would work as a disguise until I tried it, but you can see . . ." He gestured at his own face, flat black under the shadow of his hat. "It really does. You can't pick out people's features at all."

They had reached the end of the queue and Martin called up the order for thirty lots of fish and chips, causing a subdued groan from the crowd behind them. As he accepted two carrier bags full of fizzy drink cans and handed them over to Billy, Martin looked him full in the face. "I don't know. I think I'd know your eyes anywhere."

Billy ducked his head but he couldn't seem to go into hiding around Martin. The man just kept on watching. "They look very different when I wash it off."

"Now I want to see that."

Billy laughed, an unwonted giddiness adding itself to his uneasiness. He wasn't sure what Martin made of the explanation so far, nor was he completely sure what he himself felt, now he had been made to consider it. "So you see, it's a disguise thing. It's not a racist thing at all."

"Then why did you say it was complicated?"

"Well." Billy wanted to say something about how much he liked the look of Martin's face—the quick and subtle expressions, the openness of it, the way Martin's emotions seemed to shine out without artifice or concealment, and yet his eyes were full of careful thought. He wanted to compare that with the black of soot and say they were nothing alike. But that would not be an answer to Martin's question.

"Well, it's not got anything to do with race, but people *think* it has. People look at us and think we're wearing blackface for some racist reason. And is that just as bad? I mean, you look at us and you think, 'Am I being mocked?' And no, you're not, but that doesn't stop it from potentially ruining your day, you know? We can't stop everyone who looks at us from drawing their own conclusions—we can't grab them all and explain. So on the one hand, I don't want to ruin your day, and I don't want to make some guy in the crowd who *is* a racist feel good about himself. But on the other hand, this *is* what they did."

Billy accepted six paper-wrapped packages of fish and chips (plus one samosa and chips for the vegetarian Christine) and worried once more at this tangle that just didn't want to come undone. "I mean, some sides keep the face paint but use different colours, so as not to run into the problem. Red Leicester use red, for example, and red would work with our kit too."

Martin's smile had fallen. He looked thoughtful and a little sad, and Billy felt wretched over it.

"But it wouldn't be real," Martin said.

"That's it." Billy's stomach was turning over and growling with the smell of vinegar, so he couldn't be sure how much was hunger and how much was relief, but God, here was a man who spoke his language. "That's it exactly. How important is it not to lie about the past? If you're going to keep a tradition alive, and tell everyone it's something that goes back to the fifteenth century, do you have the right to change it? Do you need to change it because people look at it and see something in it that isn't actually there?"

"Or do you keep it the same, knowing that people are going to be hurt by it?"

Billy looked down helplessly at his fingertips, poking like adventurous worms out of his fingerless gloves. They were currently the only part of him where the natural colour was visible. "Yeah. And that's why it's complicated."

CHAPTER EIGHT

Complicated, Martin thought, taking off his cloak and wrapping it around the parcels of chips. Maybe it would take weeks for the smell to wear off, but it would be worth it. There was just something itchy about walking around with modern food in authenti-kit. The press seemed to love snapping pictures of Vikings with Coke bottles, and it wasn't what he wanted in the papers.

Part of him was trying to hold on to its grudge. What Billy was saying with his "complicated" was that he considered an accurate portrayal of history more important than real people's feelings. And that was patently mockable when you were talking about the history of six blokes capering about with bells on . . .

Except that Martin could see that the unpainted faces, the faces painted other colours, must do to Billy what Stigand's brooch did to him—must set off that little pedantic voice that he could not shut up that said, *But it's not right, is it? What's the point of doing it at all if you're not going to do it right?*

"Maybe that's something you can explain when you go on," he offered. "You'll have a microphone and a crowd. A good opportunity to educate them, yeah?"

Billy beamed at him, looking reprieved, and Martin found the guy's earnestness as charming as his awkwardness. He got the impression Billy was soaking up his approval—maybe just even his notice—like some sort of blessing. It was a flattering feeling.

"So . . ." Billy swung the bag full of cans over his shoulder as they headed towards Bretwalda's encampment. "Why Vikings?"

An unadventurous question, but gently put. Martin had had far more dismissiveness aimed at him in his time. "I'm mixed. My mother's a Yorkshirewoman, my father's from the Sudan."

"Right. So it's your heritage."

And the answer didn't usually get accepted so wholeheartedly as that. Martin's bullshit-meter registered low. He felt himself relaxing moment by moment out of defensive wariness and into enjoyment. There was no pressing reason then that he couldn't drop back a little and mourn the fact that the flapping jacket covered up what was surely a very nice arse.

"But what about your dad's heritage?"

"Well." Martin lifted one of the rope barriers that lined the public paths so that Billy could duck underneath them and come into Bretwalda's encampment. "A fair amount of both Saxons and Vikings travelled to Rome on pilgrimage even in the time we're reenacting, and a fair amount of Nubians travelled from the Sudan to Rome to trade in gold, ivory, and gems. No reason why a Viking couldn't have married a merchant's daughter while he was out there and brought her home. And it gives me a good chance to tell people about Kush and Nubia and the kingdom of Meroe, which none of them have heard about."

"I've heard of Kush from the Bible, and Nubian pharaohs in Egypt," Billy offered, looking around in obvious wonder at the stands of armour, the women busily weaving and embroidering, the men carving wood and stitching leather.

"Then you're already ahead of most people. Here we are."

Martin lifted a corner of the work shelter and ducked inside. There, six wooden benches had been crowded around the firebox, a massive and gorgeous thing made of two-inch-thick oak and filled with sand. It contained a fire large enough to heat two cauldrons hanging from separate tripods, or for one cauldron and a separate trivet on which (when the canvas walls of the shelter hid them from the prying eyes of the public) they could boil kettles for coffee and tea.

The benches were crowded with crow-people, as he found he still thought of Billy's troupe. They didn't look so threatening now he knew about the soot. He was able to return the smiles offered to him with genuine affability as he handed out food.

"This stuff is amazing." Billy looked around in awe, touching antler-handled knives, wrought iron cookware, and pole lathe turned bowls and cups. Giving him his lunch, Martin checked all the cauldrons, found water in the third, and made tea in a Stamford ware cup for Billy and in his own replica Merotic cup with the flying snakes for himself.

"Most people are disappointed." Martin sank down with some relief to his own bench. It looked like the dancers had been made welcome. Edith was sitting next to Mrs. Cleveland, listening to some story about the war. Everyone had tea, now they all had food, and no one—not even the beanpole—looked snooty anymore. Crisis averted.

"Why?"

"They want us half-naked in furs and gold and barbarian splendour. Preferably with horned helmets and two-handed swords, strapped on our backs, no less, like cheap knock-off copies of Conan."

"Ha, yes." The redhaired guy who had broken out in unexpected martial arts earlier had an ox horn full of coffee and looked right at home. "Fantasy history. We were just saying on the way here that that was a problem of ours. The real thing never looks quite as impressive as the public seems to hope."

Billy abandoned the three-legged stool he had been sitting on, and squeezed himself onto the bench next to Martin. He smelled of brandy and beer. The press of his hip and the long toned muscles of his thigh against Martin's were as hot and intoxicating as his smell. Martin wriggled, ostensibly to give Billy room, but actually to press their knees more firmly together. He was pretty sure this was blatant encouragement on Billy's part, pretty sure he wasn't just mistaking the signs because it was still frustratingly difficult to read that featureless face.

"That's what we find too," he agreed, shrugging. "But it's not really our problem, is it? We put the information out there, and we're all here to be talked to. All of us can answer the most common questions, or find someone in the society who knows, even if we don't. We're here to teach, for those who want to learn. If the rest of them want to stay ignorant, that's their look out, am I right?"

Billy laughed at that. As he put his empty chip paper in the fire, he leaned in closer to Martin to say in an undertone, "But I wouldn't mind seeing you half-naked in furs."

Martin almost spat out his tea. A great wash of heat flashed through him, half-arousal and half-embarrassment. He turned, intending to hiss, "You can't say that kind of thing *here*," at Billy, but couldn't get it out. Billy was industriously studying the grass beneath the firebox, with the hunched shoulders and tiny incredulous smile of a man who couldn't believe what he'd just said.

"Pillock," Martin said instead, and shoved him in the arm in a friendly, manly sort of way, in lieu of knocking him to the ground and climbing on top. One day Bretwalda would be a place where he could do that sort of thing, but today was not that day.

CHAPTER
NINE

Lunch eaten, the Griffins excused themselves to go and poke around the fete for an hour before they had to perform in the arena. Billy lagged behind, and Martin noticed how easily he was left, as though he had become invisible as soon as his friends' backs were turned. Billy didn't seem to mind, only smiled at Martin, obviously trying to think of something to say and failing.

"I'm going down to have a talk to the bloke on that stall about selling our people out-of-period tat," Martin announced to the members of his garrison who were listening, although postlunch torpor meant that most of them were asleep in the shade at this point. Having covered himself with a believable excuse, he joined Billy outside the encampment's ropes. "Shall we look around together?"

"I'd like that."

So they spent a very pleasant hour strolling past archery butts and racks of animated toys, doughnut shops and fudge shops, and four kebab vans in a row. By mutual consent a good half hour was spent in the bar tent, trying each other's beers. And though Billy still didn't say much, his presence seemed to crackle by Martin's side like lightning in a bottle.

They bought doughnuts, and Martin was just luxuriating in the way Billy stood so close to him while they ate when Billy leaned forward and with his teeth took the final morsel of dough out of Martin's mouth. Martin choked in surprise, had to bend double and heave for breath, then wash his scraped throat cool with the last of his beer.

Billy stepped back, eyes wide and his hands raised. "I'm sorry; I thought you were interested. I can't . . . I can't say these things; I have to—"

Martin scrambled to get himself back together before they had a misunderstanding. "Yes. God! Yes, I am interested. Don't run away."

Oh, he hated that face paint. He couldn't see whether Billy's expression was anger or just confusion.

"I . . . too fast?"

And that made him laugh. "Sorry. It's just a bit public." Martin waved a hand at his armour, his sword in its scabbard. "And also I'm going for 'big scary Viking' here. It doesn't go with the image."

It was clearly Billy's turn to be caught between suspicion and anger, Martin thought, judging from the sarcastic tone of his voice as he said, "There were never any gay Vikings?"

"Oh, well, there were, but if you bottomed, you were kind of despised. You wouldn't have an equal partnership. Owner and slave, maybe, or warrior and captive—which is much the same thing."

Martin had slipped into lecturing mode, which was not at all appropriate for a conversation in which a potential boyfriend was wondering if you were ashamed of him. He turned it back towards the personal, as far as he could. "But yes, the truth is that I've got a new society to hold together and I stand out enough for the colour of my skin without having any more minority ticky boxes against me. I'm just . . . waiting for a better time to tell the rest of the garrison. When things aren't quite so precarious."

Billy smiled and dropped the hand he'd apparently raised to tug at Martin's wrist. "Things never do get less precarious, in my experience. But then, I can afford to think that because five minutes after I say anything they all forget I'm there anyway. I don't matter enough to be homophobic about."

"Of course you matter." Martin unearthed his watch from his pouch. "Shit, you're on in ten minutes. Come on. I can't let you miss your spot a second time."

Back with two minutes to spare, Billy took the pudgy guy—his name was Matt, Martin remembered—aside for a moment to whisper fiercely in his ear. They both looked at Martin, then back again, and Matt nodded as he took the microphone.

Some good-humoured laughter greeted the Griffins when they finally walked out into the exhibition ring, as though morris dancing by its very nature was an in-joke shared among friends. Edith had provided Mrs. Cleveland with a fold-up leather stool so that she could sit to play the drum. It lay by her feet, appreciated for the thought, but unwanted.

Matt launched into his opening spiel. "Ladies and gentlemen and others, we are the Stomping Griffins, and we're going to dance for you some dances that go back five hundred years. People will tell you that this is an ancient pagan tradition, but that's frankly untrue. People will tell you women never danced the morris; that's a myth put about by the Victorians. People will tell you we black our faces to frighten away the evil spirits, which is bollocks too. Let me tell you why we do that, and then we'll start our set with 'Room for the Cuckolds'. And kids, if you want to know what a cuckold is, ask your parents..."

They were good, Martin thought in some surprise, after the second dance had proved the first was no fluke. He hadn't expected that level of concern for their appearance to go with actual competence. But there was something crisp and smart about the way the straight lines of three men combined into circles, slanted into diamonds, burst out into swirls and spirals only to recombine into the basic rectangle as if by magic.

Nothing effete about the dance. When those sticks clashed, wood would splinter and fly. At one point, the whole top of Graham's stick was severed to encouraging laughter and ribald comments from the side. Billy danced with vigour, combining strength and lightness in a smooth practised style that made the less talented dancers look lumpen and jerky.

When the side came on, it had been to good-humoured condescension, the onlookers clearly thinking that, like sprouts at Christmas, you had to have the morris but you didn't have to like it. By the end of the last dance, the crowd was cheering, nicely warmed up for Bretwalda.

Martin got the garrison lined up to go on. The Griffins ambled off in a shambolic mass, leaving Matt, still providing commentary, Billy, and the fiddle player alone in the centre of the ring.

Matt bowed to the crowd. "Some of you may have been watching earlier when we had a little altercation with the next chaps outside the ring. I have to say that's not our normal style at all. *This* is how a morris dancer throws down a challenge..."

Matt walked off. The fiddler began to play, standing with her black greatcoated back to Bretwalda as though she didn't acknowledge their existence. Billy, facing the fiddler, was also facing Martin. He had taken off his jacket to reveal a long, slender torso in a white linen shirt. His bright-blue gaze lifted and locked on Martin's as he stood loosely, head up, waiting for the music to give him his cue.

What was all this then?

Billy began to dance: leaping, stepping, stamping, his feet beating against the ground as if sounding a kettledrum. Those long legs were graceful and powerful, his arms raised and balanced and bright against the blue sky. Martin couldn't see the expression on his face even now, but his body was clearly boasting about its own prowess. *I'm faster, lighter, stronger than you. I can jump higher and endure longer. You want virile? Look at me.*

And damn, it was effective. He was the most beautiful creature Martin had ever seen, with sweat dampening that white shirt and turning it translucent, his grin all challenge and his laughing gaze never varying from Martin's face.

With two great bounds forward, Billy fell to one knee in front of Martin, his arms spread wide, red handkerchiefs dangling from his hands like flags. Martin looked down, embarrassed and aroused and singled out, as though he had just been propositioned in front of the summer crowd.

Billy raised his eyebrows. "Top that."

Oh, he was on. Martin leaned down to give him a single stage direction. "Run."

He began to clash his spear against his shield, making a hollow, wooden drumbeat. Used to this, the garrison echoed the sound in a slow handclap of weapons designed to psych the enemy out. Billy's grin narrowed, became conspiratorial. He got to his feet, made a show of looking Martin up and down as if only just realizing what he was up against.

Sword slid from scabbard. Martin stepped forward and bellowed a war cry into Billy's face. Billy leapt four feet in the air, turned, and came down running. To the welcome sound of the entire audience roaring with laughter, Martin gave pursuit. But he had barely made it into the centre of the ring before fleet-footed Billy had hurdled over the straw bales at the outer edge and disappeared.

Martin's wishes were granted. It was indeed a good battle. Ulf and Stigand came off with their faces glowing, having lived through the whole thing and "killed" at least one man each. Athelstan hadn't braced his shield hard enough against an oncoming axe blow, and the shield's edge had been knocked back into his face. It had caught him just above the eyebrow and split the skin. But the cut was only a centimetre across, easily fixed by the St. John's ambulance later, and the pouring blood was a crowd-pleaser. Athelstan himself had made sure to bleed over the white-painted hide cover of his shield and was visibly proud of the spatter effect he'd achieved.

Martin came off equally elated. He looked around for Billy, hoping for praise, but the Griffins were nowhere to be found. Disappointed, he checked the programme for tomorrow, and found out that they were only here for one day, their place in the programme for Sunday taken up by a local samba band.

They'd gone. They'd gone, right in the middle of Bretwalda's display, without even saying good-bye.

The organizer came over, sufficiently unstressed now to actually have his hat on his head. "That was brilliant, mate. Really glad we put you on last—send the crowd home with a bang, you know. You do that again tomorrow, and we can sign up to you coming back next year, no problem."

Martin wrestled down the disappointment long enough to give a convincing impression of someone who was as delighted as he should be, and shook the man's hand on it.

Damn.

A seat by the fire beckoned, in the middle of a throng of happy people. The fretfulness of this morning was wiped from the mind as the warriors retold their moments of glory while dinner simmered appetizingly in the great cauldrons.

"There's hot water for coffee." Edith picked the wooden lid off the smallest cauldron and showed him steaming water pricked with bubbles. "What's up?"

Martin sighed and went to uncover the bowls in the back of the shelter which concealed coffee granules and sugar. With a spoonful of each in his mug, and milk from the jug, he returned to ladle water out of the pan on top. "Oh, I don't know..." *I just thought maybe there was something going to happen there. I was so sure.* "Tired, I guess."

"Dinner's not going to be ready for another couple of hours. I need someone to chop more wood, and the carrots." She shrugged. "Why don't you go and have a nap?"

"Yeah," he agreed, more knocked back than a few hours' acquaintance should justify. *I never even got to see his face.* "I might do that."

"That bloke from the morris dancers came by to give me back my stool," she added, stopping him just as he turned for his tent.

"Oh yes?"

"Said he was sorry they had to go but one of them had to get back for a meeting, and they were all in one minibus. He put the cup you loaned him back in your tent."

Martin could see the beaker Billy had used on the table next to the butter churn. His heart gave a hopeful little caper. "Right."

Sure enough, when he had searched his tent for barely five minutes, he found the chip receipt curled up in the right foot of his spare set of shoes. On it Billy had written, *We must do this again. Phone me*, and left not only his number but also his home address.

His day transformed, Martin put the note in his pouch for safekeeping and went back out to chop carrots before Edith tried again to get Kayleigh to do it.

CHAPTER TEN

Billy's more worrying lodger was fumbling at the front door when he cycled home.

"Here, let me," he said, pulling out his own keys and leaning over the silver boxes Kaminski had stacked on the porch. Hard metal boxes with locks, just like the toffs had used on the rabbit shoot. Billy could still feel the weight of them in his hands, and the reminder turned him cold.

Unlocking and pushing open the door, he tried not to be distressed or surprised when Kaminski barged straight in without even nodding at him. Kaminski was used to him coming in and out in morris kit by now, so he didn't expect surprise. But a basic acknowledgement might have been nice. "Can I help you carry some of this?"

They looked just like ammunition boxes. And that hard case with the carrying strap to go over a shoulder, also metal, also lockable, was just the right size for two rifles, or one of something a bit more sinister. A machine gun could probably fit in that thing.

"No need." Kaminski gave him a glower, hot as an arc welder, and snatched the boxes from under Billy's curious hands before he could test their weight by picking them up. "I have it."

"I could help bring them in?"

"You will not touch my things. I add more locks."

Billy didn't believe in judging someone by how they looked, but it was hard to ignore the fact that Kaminski had the physique of a boxer and the dented face of a rugby player. His nose must have been broken at least twice to achieve such spread, and his cauliflower ears stood out painfully red from the blond stubble of his skinhead hair cut. Tattoos squirmed from beneath the collar and cuffs of his crisp white shirt, wormed like ivy up his neck, down his wrists and onto the backs of his hands.

"Okay." Billy raised both hands in surrender. "That's fine. I will need to be able to get back into your part of my house if you leave, though, so don't make the place too impenetrable."

"It will not be a problem." Kaminski levered the box that looked just like a gun case through his door, followed it with the ammunition boxes, and stood for a moment, watching Billy with eyes like blue lasers as Billy brought in his bike and locked the front door behind him. Then he disappeared into his own room, and Billy heard the sound of three locks and five bolts being secured. Then the muffled sound of some Polish or Russian radio station.

Billy took his bike upstairs, leaving Kaminski in full control of the ground floor.

The house had belonged to the Wrights as long as anyone could remember, so the mortgage had long been paid off, but the rent from two lodgers was the mainstay of Billy's income. He couldn't afford to ask Kaminski to leave just because he found the guy terrifying. Apart from occasional bleed-throughs of Russian radio melodrama through the floor at 2 a.m., he paid his rent on time, was no trouble at all and . . .

. . . was exactly the kind of model tenant you'd expect of a Russian mafia mobster trying to avoid being noticed by the police.

That's ridiculous. You're being ridiculous to think such a thing. It's hardly Kaminski's fault that you're such a coward, so oversensitive, overdramatic, and prone to freaking out like a sissy when anything harder than yourself—which is frankly everything in the world—crosses your path.

Parking his bike on his own landing, Billy listened for the state of affairs in the flat above his. About this time . . . ah yes. A chorus of high-pitched yipping broke out over his head. The sound of hard nails scrabbling on floorboards heralded the four West Highland terriers running over to their food bowls. Then came the inevitable growls and injured squeaks as they battled for who ate first, and the groan of the old plumbing as Mrs. Webb filled a dog bowl with water and put that down among them.

Three times a week or so he would run up the stairs and look in on them. Mrs. Webb would be seated in her flowery print dress, overflowing her chair, knitting. These days the dogs had stopped hurling themselves at Billy like hairy torpedoes the moment he opened the door. Now they just raised their heads from where they lay, one on her knee, one on her feet, two on the window ledge like cats.

It smelled a little in there, and she looked at him with a kind of desperation, as though she'd always told herself she wouldn't allow her life to end up like this. She couldn't get out now, couldn't get back up the stairs if she got down them, or walk into town if she did come down. Billy guessed she was more invisible than he was, that if he stopped seeing her, she might fade away altogether.

One day, if they were kept properly fed, he would hear the dogs howling and go up to find she was dead in that chair. If they were not properly fed, he didn't want to think about what might happen. So he always got her groceries when he got his own now, always listened out, just to be sure. Always hated going up there because he knew she could tell what he was thinking. They both knew what the inevitable end would be.

He closed his own door on the stairwell and locked the depressing thoughts outside, trying to stave off his inevitable crash for as long as possible. Taking off his top hat, he set it on the polystyrene head he kept for that purpose on the top of the bookshelf. The bubble of energy he had managed to summon up to keep the dark away had thinned into a second skin by this point. The fatigue of a sleepless night and the highs of a good dance-out felt like a fragile defence against the monstrous amorphous thing that was prowling under his breastbone and in his lungs, waiting to strike, waiting to suck all the colour and the pleasure out of his life.

But it hadn't closed in yet, and he was going to savour the unexpected brilliance of today with every moment he still had. He stripped off his kit, hanging up the heavy tattered jacket, putting the sweaty shirt and trousers in the washing basket.

The sink in his bathroom had been used to wash off so much face paint the grout of the tiles had gone grey. He leaned over it to scrub today's layer loose with a couple of handfuls of Swarfega, and then turned the shower on, intending to wash mask and grime off together.

He let the water run through his hands, adjusting the temperature until it was perfect before he stepped in. The jets soaked into his hair and massaged his scalp, making his skin tingle all over as water began to sluice over his tired muscles and sticky skin.

The little cubicle filled with steam, which the last rays of sunshine lit dappled gold as they streamed almost horizontally through the window. His skin warmed and flushed under the hot rain, as he filled a hand with tea tree–scented shampoo and built up lather on his hair.

Rinsing it off, eyes closed and head thrown back, face held trustingly under the flood, the soap slid down his body, tracing a path like hands, hands all over him. He'd noticed Martin's hands, of course, square and capable. He'd noticed them as they gestured in enthusiasm, as they clenched around the hilt of that very businesslike sword, or rifled with practised deftness through the stacks of forms his underlings kept giving him.

His hands had looked strong. Almost against Billy's will, he felt them touch him, ghost touches, as he imagined what it might be like if Martin were in here with him, strong hands stroking down his back while the man looked at him. He'd look just as he had when Billy danced for him—he'd look possessive and proud and just a tad predatory, with that little spark of something that said, *You're mine.*

Billy slid his own hands down his soapy chest, his eyes shut, Martin's face close in his mind. He could almost feel the warmth from Martin's skin, breath on his ear as Martin leaned in to touch. "Mmm," he said and arched his back, pressing his hips up against the body he was imagining in here with him, naked and wet as he was.

His fantasy faltered slightly there. Even out of his armour, Martin had been hard to check out. Viking clothes seemed to run to the modest, big ballooning trousers under long skirted tunics with long sleeves concealing everything. Martin's arms had been covered in silver bracelets over the red wool of his tunic, but with two layers of cloth beneath them, they'd done nothing to show muscle definition, just made him look bulkier.

But bulky was something. The guy had broad shoulders, his throat strong with muscle. He might be cut under there, with every muscle defined and rippling, not an inch of fat on him, or he might just be solid—the kind of shape created by nature rather than the gym, a kind of rocklike, unshakeable heaviness. Billy would be happy with either. He slid a soapy hand over his chest, over his nipples, humming at the sweet blush of pleasure that brought. Not enough. When he did it again, he dragged his nails over them, just lightly, just enough to turn the sweetness of the response into a sharper sting.

It occurred to him to wonder if he should stop. If this was taking advantage. Maybe Martin wouldn't like him wanking off to the memory of him, just as he had not liked the playful come-on.

Maybe that had put the guy off him, and Martin would never phone, would throw Billy's number away and never call? Maybe he was scared Billy would accidentally out him as he had almost done with the doughnut thing? Maybe he just wasn't discreet enough for such a straight-acting macho kind of man?

Maybe he was glad to get rid of you after you made him look like an idiot, after you did a courting dance *for him in front of the whole of Trowchester. Maybe you make him sick.*

Shut up!

Squeezing his eyes closed, Billy rinsed the last dregs of the foam away, hesitated, and then reached for the shower gel again.

Maybe Martin never would call. Then he wouldn't have to know.

He took a best guess at Martin's figure, imagined the guy, stocky and strong, crowding the little stall, water sliding between them as Martin reached around Billy to stroke callused hands down over his spine, lower into the small of his back and over the curve of his buttocks. Billy tilted his head, craned his throat forward to meet Martin's imaginary kisses, could almost feel the slow sucking bites as they bruised his neck.

With one soapy hand, he reached behind himself to stroke a blunt fingertip across his hole, coaxing a deep, intimate velvety need out of himself. Martin would do that. Martin would prepare him gently but . . . inexorably. There wouldn't be any doubt. No tentativeness. He could surrender to Martin's control and know that all the decisions were in good hands.

He could . . . With the other hand, he stroked for the first time along his hard, aching cock. No, no, he didn't. Martin did. He was pressed against the tiles, supported by Martin's weight; Martin's hand, curled as it had been around the hilt of his sword, deft and stroking... just like that, perfectly.

Billy's hips twitched forwards, urging him to speed the pace even as he forced himself to slow it down. He twisted in the steamy heat, trying to get more than a fingertip into himself. It wasn't working. In this position his arms just weren't long enough.

More soap. He slicked himself all over, kneeling in the pounding spray. With his head lower than his arse, water ran up his back and into his hair, licking over his skin. He imagined the touch was Martin's many braids loosed from their tie. If he concentrated hard, he could almost feel the weight against his back, feel Martin's limbs enfold him like another, stronger bubble, like Martin might even be able to keep it all away, the cold and the dark, just by the power in his stocky frame.

This was better. Billy's middle finger sunk in to the knuckle even as the water tapped over his arsehole, tickling like a vibrator. He sped up the hand on his prick and added a second finger. Oh God, that was...

What would he sound like? Would he lean in close and whisper filthy things, his breath hot in Billy's ear? Or would he just take the earlobe in his mouth and suck as he pushed himself deep into Billy's body, solid and protective and so slow, so unrelentingly...

"Oh please," Billy gasped, forgetting for a moment that he was alone. He undulated between the two different sources of bliss, back into aching penetration and forward into a sharp, triumphant pleasure as his balls clenched like a fist against him. "Oh please, Martin!" and he came over the wet floor of the shower, his mouth hanging open, hot water pounding on his stinging hole.

He managed to keep the illusion a moment longer, feeling Martin's nose nuzzle behind his ear, trying to imagine words of praise and reassurance in the low, smooth voice. But he couldn't quite bring any to mind.

We both know it's never going to happen. Because he forgot you the moment you were out of sight. Let's face it, who wouldn't?

Shut up!

Laboriously he got his feet under himself, suddenly aware of how sordid he must look, how pathetic, jerking himself off in the shower because he was not fit to have a relationship with a real person.

Who would put up with you? Even you despise yourself.
He braced his hand on the slippery tiles of the wall and pushed himself to his feet, his legs shaking and his knees loose under him. The cold thoughts and the clench around his heart, the fist of lead that squeezed it so tight he could hardly breathe, were familiar and unwelcome. He fought them with everything he had, sluicing himself clean, turning off the water, and hastily towelling body and hair. If he was going to crash, it would be better to do it dressed and dry.

There was dinner to be made, emails to be answered. Maybe if he didn't listen to his inner hater, if he reestablished some structure in his day, ate something, washed up, like a normal, capable person, he could keep it away for the rest of today.

Certainly, if he gave in to it, if he let it get bad, he'd end up as he had been the first time he lost his job—lying in bed all day long, an absence wrapped in useless skin. Regardless of whether he ever saw Martin again, he didn't want that.

Clean, he dressed in real-person clothes, made a coffee, and put a pan of pasta on to boil, rustling up a simple sauce out of canned tomatoes, chopped onion, and dried mixed herbs. Outside, the summer evening blued towards night. His kitchen window, at the back of the house, faced the village church over a field of green-gold barley, and the starlings were tracing fluid shapes over the steeple, moving as one strange entity, like a school of black fish in the air.

The steeple clock said twelve minutes past three, but it always did. Inside a hedge of blackthorn, the tumbled gravestones slept beneath cornflowers and long grass, and the dog roses glowed like rubies where they clambered up the inevitable ancient yew trees. Evening was crystallising over all of them with a heavy golden light, preserving this moment as if in amber.

Sad suddenly, Billy took his meal into the small sitting room and switched on both TV and laptop. *Time Team* was on, talking about an archaeological dig somewhere in the Mendips, cutting back through the soil of a hump in a farmer's field, finding tools and animal bones from the Bronze Age, when the quiet agricultural landscape had been a ceremonial site, a temple to some god whose name no one would ever again know.

Billy ate his pasta, and wondered about going down to the Albert, where conversation would probably not revolve around the impermanence of things, the inevitability that even if you weren't a ghost now you would soon become one. That someone else would dance your dances and flaunt themselves in your jigs because you'd had your chance and you had flubbed it.

Sometimes, if there were five men present and it was a six-man dance, the side would dance around the space where the absent dancer should be as if the space was occupied. It was called "dancing with a ghost." Billy smiled painfully at the thought. Maybe that was what they felt like when he was there—that he was a nothing outlined in black.

Just stop it, all right? He could feel himself slipping towards the pit, his breathing going shallow around the clench of a dark universe in his chest. It was still a good day—he couldn't get the thing out of him, but the tilt of the floor was shallow enough that he could dig his mental fingers in and slow the slide towards it.

He switched *Time Team* off, waded conscientiously through three-quarters of his dinner, ignored the call of the beer bottles in the kitchen—the only alcohol allowed in the house—in favour of making St. John's wort tea and eating a slab of dark chocolate. The internet failed him. No one had emailed. None of the blogs he followed had anything interesting to say, and he didn't think he could face cat pictures just at the moment.

You had a great day. You met someone interesting, who liked you.

Yeah, but he didn't, though.

He'll call you. He just can't do it now because he's in a field that has no reception.

He won't call. He's forgotten me already.

Maybe if you made more of an effort . . .

To be someone I'm not?

Yes. Maybe if you were someone else, everyone would like you.

Well, thanks for that wonderful advice. You're fucking useless.

I know. I know I am.

Having reached its inevitable end point, the train of thought derailed for a moment. It was still a good day because Billy could get off at that point and look for a book to distract him. He got in almost ten minutes of browsing titles before it started up again.

Maybe if you weren't so useless.
God, I hate you sometimes. Shut up!
Other people don't stand in their living room arguing with themselves over how hateful they are. Other people manage to choose a book when they set out to choose a book. Other people—

A buzz, like the hum of a hornet the size of his head, interrupted his thoughts. The doorbell was ringing. Billy's internal dialogue fell into a surly mutter at the back of his mind as claws scrabbled across the ceiling and four high-pitched doggy voices yammered protest overhead. From downstairs a cello concerto was amplified into magnificence as Mr. Kaminski turned the volume up, either to protest the intrusion or to ignore it.

For a moment, Billy didn't stir. He had enough to do. Couldn't the universe see that he was fighting for his sanity here? He didn't have the energy left over to go down and open doors to strangers. He'd had a whole day of people and noise and interaction, and he *could not deal* with any more of it.

The buzz came again, reproachful and insistent, putting up his hackles like a violin piece played slightly off-key. Would it never shut up?

Well, no. It wouldn't because Kaminski *wouldn't* answer the door and Mrs. Webb *couldn't*. If the noise was to be stopped, it would have to be stopped by Billy. He bowed his head, took two deep breaths, firmly shut the blast doors on the black hole in his chest, and went to do it himself.

He trudged down the stairs, through the hall, his bare feet cold on the Victorian tiles. The Yale lock was stubbornly difficult as he fumbled with it, that or there was some disconnect between his brain and his hand.

Finally he twisted the little knob and pulled the door open far enough to admit the night, the wind scented of green wheat and . . . burning? There was a silhouette he didn't recognise on the step, cut out of the steel-washed moonlit sky. "Hello?"

Stepping forward into the light from the hall, Martin grinned and held out a bottle of Elgood's Golden Newt ale. He looked quite different in real-person clothes, only the smell of woodsmoke left to suggest he had been living in the ninth century this morning.

This wasn't possible. Billy stood quite still as his sluggish thoughts tried to wrap themselves around the vision.

"It is Billy Wright, yes?" Martin leaned forward, his smile broadening. He took Billy by the chin and turned his face to the light of a distant streetlamp. "I'm sure it is. The face is new to me, but I'd recognise those legs anywhere."

CHAPTER ELEVEN

"Martin?" When Billy looked at his watch, it said half eleven. It felt as though a dozen days had come and gone since this afternoon, and for a moment he couldn't connect up the flirting and the dancing with this place, this very modern man.

In another universe, he thought he might be overcome with joy. Certainly something tried to leap up at the back of his mind, and fell, too heavy to take flight. Certainly a part of him wanted to bound and beam and exclaim with joy because he'd been so sure Martin wouldn't want anything more to do with him that he'd begun to think of the man as a myth, and now he was here. Real and alive and actually here. Presumably because he had liked Billy too.

He fell back on pleasantries while his mind caught up. "Come in."

In the glow of the hall, Martin was a sight to see. Shorter than Billy, but compact, the cut-off arms of his Metallica T-shirt displaying wide muscular shoulders, the taper of a broad back. His jeans fitted snugly to sturdy, strong legs and a fantastic arse. Billy took it all in like gulps of water, cataloguing it for later use.

Martin had taken the tie from his hair, and the many thin braids framed his face, softening it. He looked a lot friendlier without the Viking aura enveloping him in the brutal splendour of ancient days. A little seed of life unfurled into the void in Billy's chest at the sight. His breath came deeper and easier as he smiled.

"I thought you'd be stuck in your field for the weekend."

"They're rehashing the battle of Hastings." Martin followed him up the stairs, looking around with interest and no apparent disapproval. "I've heard it all before."

"So you thought you'd drive for an hour to come and visit me?"

Martin's smile broadened. "Yes," he said, as though it was the simplest thing in the world. "I was afraid if I let you get away, someone else would move in before I got the chance."

It was so absurd, Billy couldn't truly believe it. But it was nice to hear all the same. He got out the glasses from under the sink and poured the beer, conscious that he was not coming across as the man Martin had met. Conscious of being awkward and silent and twitchy.

Because you met him when you were on an up, and he thinks you're this bright-eyed, doe-like, springy, confident, charming creature, and as soon as he figures out what you're really like, he'll be gone. And maybe it would have been better if he hadn't turned up at all. You could have pretended for longer that you and he might have . . .

"Was that a bad idea?" Martin peered out of the window, over to where the church's porch light was casting a creepy blue glimmer over the graveyard. His smile had changed shape in a way that perhaps indicated distress. "I mean, it was kind of forward?"

"It wasn't." Billy could see how the evening would fail. He would either not say enough, or he would overcompensate and say too much. Martin would get the impression that he wasn't really wanted, and leave. After which he would never come back.

Trying to forestall the inevitable, he stepped forward and wound both hands around Martin's forearm. A good move. He liked the feel of it, bare skin over muscle, warm with today's stored sunshine and with life. "It was a great idea. I can't believe you'd— I mean, I'm really grateful. I don't deserve . . . and you're so . . ."

Oh God, this was pathetic. He blew out a frustrated breath and tried again, still anchored to Martin's arm, as if pulling on Martin's strength to formulate his thoughts. "I'm sorry; I just, I crash, you know. When the day's too good, or I dance too hard, or something trips me up."

As if this wasn't the death knell of any relationship, and rightly so. Why should anyone have to deal with this if it wasn't hardwired into their own brain? "I get depressed, and—"

Martin covered Billy's hands with his own, his look of disappointment shading into something warmer, surprisingly sympathetic. "You want me to go while you get yourself together?"

"No! No, I just. Want to apologise, I guess. I won't be as much fun as maybe you hoped."

Billy freed a hand to pick up a glass of beer and take a sip. His self-reproach was interrupted by the realization that this was some good stuff, light, almost citrussy on the sides of the tongue, with a flowering of unexpected depth and complexity at the back of the throat, hops and oak and grapefruit. He could actually taste it, which told him he was not quite as far gone as he feared. "I'm still glad... I'm *really* glad you're here."

Surprisingly, Martin wasn't heading for the door at all. He seemed to be relaxing. He lifted the beer out of Billy's hand and set it back on the table. Then he pushed Billy, gently but firmly into the wall. His kiss was just as Billy had hoped: no doubt behind it but very little pressure either. Not coercing him, but not needing any persuasion.

Billy could feel the kiss too. The pleasure was distant, but it was there. He pushed back and bit down a little, sliding his hands around Martin's waist, getting them up under his T-shirt to explore the corded strength of his back and dip towards the swell of his buttocks. Not sure if the touch would be appreciated, if it was allowed, if he was doing it right. How long he'd be allowed to go on until Martin realized he wasn't worth the effort and stopped him.

Martin just pressed in closer, and though part of Billy's unruly mind was still drowned under despair, like a deserted village under a reservoir's waters, certain other parts of himself registered yearning, hopeless want.

"How d'you feel about making out on the sofa?"

Billy dropped his head onto Martin's shoulder. What he really needed was bed, to lie down and curl into the other man's warmth, to push his face into Martin's neck and close his eyes and be held until sleep came. If he could do that, it was not impossible that he would wake with enough energy to be cheerful and sexy and responsive in the morning. It seemed too complicated to explain. "Straight to bed?"

Martin kissed the outside edges of his closed eyes, combed his fingers through Billy's loose curls. "Are you sure you really want that, Prancer? Because you look like death warmed up, to be honest."

He didn't sound too angry or too cheated to stay. This was not going at all how Billy had imagined it. For a start, Martin's arms were still wrapped around him, his weight pressing into Billy's chest, holding him against the wall. While he wasn't sure if he actually had the strength in him for sex, he was damn certain that at this stage, when Martin came to his senses and left, it was going to be all but impossible to rein in the desire to plead with him to come back.

"I'm just so tired. I'm sorry. I know this isn't what you wanted. I know I come across more . . . when I'm in a mask. But come to bed? Don't leave?"

If he had been Martin, he'd have been out of the door now. Running out, his heart thundering, like anyone would who'd gone after a pretty face only to find the monsters behind it, all teeth and despair. He wasn't going to blame the man, if that was how he reacted. How could he? The blame belonged right here on Billy's messed-up head.

If only Martin had waited a couple of days, phoned him on an upswing, given him the chance to meet up when he could pretend to be a normal human being.

If only. Yeah, well he was depressed enough without dwelling on that.

"Okay," said Martin, which made no sense. Billy found himself being manhandled across the room to where the door of his bedroom stood open, his unmade bed looking slovenly, a great barometer of a man who couldn't muster the willpower to smooth down a duvet in the morning.

Was he really not being rejected? That didn't compute. It raised the lid of the crypt inside which he was buried alive and let in a brief gleam of light.

If Martin wasn't leaving, perhaps Billy should attempt to look eager. He nosed Martin's hair aside and kissed his ear, worked his way down the man's throat in little biting exploratory kisses. He liked the smell of the other man, under the woodsmoke. He liked the heat of his pulse, the texture of his skin.

Martin peeled Billy out of his shirt and skimmed appreciative hands over his sides, his back. Pushing him down onto the bed, Martin unbuckled his belt, unzipped his trousers, and drew them off, pausing with a breath of rueful laughter at the sight of him, unaroused, limp, and sleepy.

Billy turned his face into the pillows, ashamed, and waited to be left.

"I thought not." Straightening up by the bedside, Martin gazed down on him. He was still smiling, for some reason, a smile that looked exasperated and fond and uncertain. "Well, this is what I get for being a presumptuous idiot, right? I should have phoned you to see if you were up to visitors before I just turned up on the doorstep. Are you sure you want me to stay?"

Billy couldn't understand why he hadn't been left already. By the magic of dodgy neurochemistry, gratitude transformed into anguish in his heart. He squeezed his eyes closed to keep it inside and could not find the willpower to ask again for what he wanted. "Do whatever you like."

He heard how that sounded—ugly, dismissive—and bit his lip to stop the prickle of tears from filling up his eyes. There was a long moment of darkness during which he tried to feel nothing. Then he heard the faint hiss of clothes being dragged over skin, and the bed creaked and dipped beside him.

Billy was bare but for boxers. When Martin snugged up tight to him, spooning against his back, pushing a leg between his, one arm under his neck and one wrapped around his waist, he could feel the heat of the other man's body all over him like sunshine. Something loosened inside, and that little seed of hope put out a green shoot.

Martin's breath warmed the back of his neck. A sense of peace, of sanctuary, welled out from all the places where they touched.

He came all this way to see you, and you let him down. Now he already knows what a loser you are. He probably already thinks you're worthless. "I'm sorry."

"Hey." Martin's hand grazed down his stomach and curled in protection and inquiry around his soft, uninterested prick. The warmth of his palm was pleasant and the tenderness of the gesture was nothing he had ever imagined encountering in his life. "Don't be. It's not your fault. I know about depression a little. My sister gets it. You on anything for it? Pills, I mean. Something I can get you?"

"It'll be better in the morning. I hope. I'll make it worth your while in the morning."

Martin laughed, his voice a deep, smooth oceanic wave of sound that lifted Billy even as he pulled him closer. Sleep began to ease apart the plastic zip ties currently strangling his heart.

"I get to spend the night with a gorgeous bloke in my arms." Martin tucked the duvet more firmly into his shoulder. "And I got to see your face. It's already been worth my while."

CHAPTER TWELVE

Martin awoke, feeling like everything had stopped. He was a long way away from the worrying decisions he had to make at work, and he was also a long way away from all the pressures of Bretwalda. He loved the group, not to put too fine a point on it. It was his baby and his pride, but shit, there was so much that needed to be done, and he ended up doing it all.

But this morning all the responsibilities he took on because someone had to if anyone was going to have any fun had been lifted off his back. It was dark behind his closed eyes—too dark for the inside of a white canvas tent on a summer morning, and the bed was too firm and too supportive for an air mattress that had been losing pressure all night long. He cracked open an eye as memory reengaged, and found that Billy had turned away from him in the night and lay on his side on the very edge of the bed, ceding Martin all the space and the duvet.

Billy looked very young there, curled like a child in the womb, his long limbs slender and coltish, his skin blued by the predawn light. Young and vulnerable.

Martin wondered what he was getting into. His sister Sheena had her depression pretty much under control now with medicine and self-help groups, but reaching a normal level of functioning was still a struggle that took up most of her daily energy. She'd changed her diet, changed her habits, given up any number of things she loved, structured her life around the illness so that she could manage it rather than letting it manage her. And still he felt the need to call every week, check with her husband that she was coping with the constant pressure of desolation on her shoulders.

Did Martin want to take on another such responsibility, given how much harder it was to hide who he was, from his father, from the school, from Bretwalda, when he was in a relationship? If he didn't, then this would be the point to slide out of bed, throw his clothes on, and disappear. And yes, that would be a pretty awful thing to do to a guy who was as on the edge as Billy was, but it would be easier on both of them than doing it later, after Billy had begun to expect him to stay.

Billy looked cold as well as young. He'd let Martin take all the covers as though even in sleep he didn't think he deserved them. Martin reached out a hand and touched the guy's bare back. It was as chill as if he'd been sleeping in the fridge. Martin couldn't have that. Carefully and quietly, he leaned in, got an arm around Billy's waist, and drew the curled-up form against his chest, tucking the covers around them both. Billy shifted with a little complaining grumble and turned into him, tucking his head under Martin's chin.

He was at first all elbows and knees, bony and cold, but when Martin smoothed the palm of his hand down Billy's back, across his shoulders, he gradually unfolded, his arm going around Martin's rib cage, his legs easing down until Martin could press their hips together and feel the welcome scald of an erect prick against his lap.

"Morning, springbok." He smiled and cupped his hands around Billy's arse, pulling him closer. They rubbed together in lazy contented warmth.

"Springbok?" Billy opened one eye, no longer quite so shocking a blue against his natural pallor, but still a startling brilliance. Sleep had restored his cocky smile, although Martin could now see the effort in it.

"You have to have a nickname, those are the rules."

"I suppose it's better than Prancer." Billy uncurled all the way, stretching up until he could mouth at Martin's neck, interspersing licks and gentle bites along the muscle and up the hinge of his jaw. He sucked Martin's earlobe into his mouth and pushed into him harder as Martin realized that he'd made the decision to stay without even being aware of it.

"You noticed that?" Still there was something delightfully languid about this early-morning lovemaking. Martin shifted to press more of his weight onto Billy, to feel the other man yield beneath it, Billy's legs opening so that he could lie between them. "You were a bit out of it last night, I thought. How're you feeling this morning?"

Billy screwed his eyes shut and arched up under him, effectively distracting him from the topic. "Don't ask. I don't want to get started thinking about it."

Martin could obey that instruction easily enough. He tangled his fingers in Billy's coffee-coloured curls and took possession of the other man's mouth in an exploratory kiss, opening him up. Billy responded gradually, his tongue tentatively stroking against Martin's, his lips softening, opening wider. Billy's hands tightened where they rested on Martin's hips, making him gasp for breath and ratcheting up the urgency with which they were both now moving together.

Martin slid his hands down the long elegant slope of Billy's flanks, rubbing warm circles into the slim muscles, brushing fingertips over the V of muscles at his hips, moved by the perfection of that little dint in the skin. He wormed his hands between Billy and the bed, took an arse cheek in either hand and squeezed.

Billy groaned, long and deep, his thrusts turning from languid to wanton. He shifted his weight, spoiling the rhythm. Martin was about to protest, until he opened his eyes to find Billy was wriggling out of his boxers. Martin sat up to help, and by the time he had tossed them into the distant washing basket, Billy had stretched out to reach the drawer of his bedside table and returned, his hand now dripping with lube.

A moment of intense shivery cold as Billy reached between them and slid his slick fingers up Martin's cock. "Ah!" Martin tipped his head back as cold melted into delicious warmth and suddenly everything was hot and tight and wet.

Then for a long while it was just lust and the pulse of friction against Billy's soft skin and his hard cock—long and slim like the rest of him, touchingly elegant in Martin's big fist when he reached down and squeezed them more firmly together.

Billy turned his face away when he came, and it made something in Martin's chest hurt. The guy was too beautiful to be this sad. "Hey," he said, as he wiped them both down with Billy's T-shirt and drew him once more snug against him. "Shh. You're all right. I understand. We're not going to think about feelings this morning. I'm just going to tell you you're fantastic and move on. D'you want some coffee? I'm sure I can figure out your kitchen and bring you some, if you want to lie here and snooze for a while."

Billy looked up, charmingly rumpled and concerned. "You've got to go back."

"Yes. I really ought to be back in the field before nine, so I can be in kit and going over the campsite to make sure everyone's hidden everything inauthentic away before we allow members of the public on site at ten. You know, I don't mind stuffing everyone's camping chairs out of sight in my tent, but I'll be damned if I have to clear up the beer cans all by myself."

"You do all this for fun?"

Martin had to laugh because was it really that obvious? "Well..." He rubbed at the roots of his braids where they pulled tight against his scalp. "I love the clothes, the fighting, the crafts, the sense of connecting people with their history. That's a passion of mine—I'm sure you know how it is."

He leaned down to disengage his discarded heap of clothes from Billy's. "But the group leadership? All the man management and administration, and worrying about finance and viability, and the endlessly telling people what to do and somehow having to make them actually do it? That's the part I could do without."

Dropping a kiss on the tip of Billy's nose, he slid out of bed. "Can I catch a quick shower?"

"Of course."

After the shower, he dressed. He didn't bother shaving—would have grown a beard in order to be more authentic if the Head hadn't made it quite clear that kind of look was not going to fly in her establishment. He staggered out into the kitchen to boil the kettle, and made two mugs of coffee. He'd hoped to be able to put one down on the bedside table for Billy, leave him tucked up and sleepy with a smile on his face and a final kiss, but Billy had thrown on jeans and a T-shirt and followed him, looking uncertain.

Here was another chance to leave and not come back, rule a line under this as a one-night stand, and save himself from a potential lifetime of angst. Billy handed Martin a bowl of cereal, turned away to find milk, his face still averted, not saying anything. And Martin had just about had it with being careful and responsible. So this hadn't turned out quite how he'd expected; it had still been good.

He didn't want to be sensible and say good-bye, damn it. It wasn't like he was afraid of a little hard work, and if Billy was complicated, then he also seemed worth it.

"Look." Martin took the tiny Biro out of his Swiss army knife and wrote his number and email address on top of yesterday's paper. "Will you call me tomorrow? Maybe we could meet up again during the week? As normal people, you know? Do something real-life together?"

Billy's small smile looked dazed. He untied the tablet-weave bracelet from around Martin's wrist and used it to tie back his hair. It left him with both arms around Martin's neck, and so they had to spend his remaining ten minutes just kissing, while the cereal turned to mush in its bowl.

"Yeah," said Billy at last. He opened the door for Martin and padded with him down the stairs to the hall. "That sounds nice. I'll—"

A thunderous knocking made the front door tremble on its hinges. Martin caught Billy's arm as he jumped and overbalanced on the stairs, righting him. It was 6:45 on a Sunday morning. "What the...?"

Whoever it was out there found the doorbell. They buzzed and buzzed until a cacophony of dogs started yammering overhead, and the door opposite Martin in the downstairs hall began rattling with the sound of opening bolts.

Billy raked his fingers through his flattened bedhair and opened the front door. Two policemen shoved their way inside, dark uniforms topped by reflective jackets, one of them holding out a permit or a badge or something he didn't have time enough to really see. "Mr. Kaminski?"

The bolted door swung open, and a blond pit bull of a man leaned his naked shoulders on the jamb. "You want what?"

"To come in, sir."

Billy licked his lips and gave Martin an unsettled, apologetic look, but he directed his words to the blond thug. "Are you all right, Mr. Kaminski?"

The first policeman had already squeezed past Kaminski and gone inside the downstairs flat. The second took a long look at Billy and Martin and drew his own conclusions. Martin judiciously kept his mouth shut.

"Who are you, please?" the second policeman asked Billy.

"Is my landlord."

"I live in the flat upstairs." Billy waved a hand at his landing and the bike leaning against the wall there.

"And you, sir?" Martin had to hand it to the police, they did menace and disdain very politely. Maybe without even trying.

"I'm just visiting. In fact I was going, right now, if that's okay?"

"Of course." The policeman gave him a little smile as if to say, "I see that guilty conscience of yours; you're just lucky I don't have time to investigate it." Or maybe that was Martin's paranoia. He grabbed Billy just as the second policeman went into Kaminski's flat and shut the door.

"What's *that* all about?"

"I don't know." Billy looked as unsettled as Martin felt, following him out of the door into a wash of dilute early-morning sunshine. Mist made the air almost visible, milky and luminous in the fresh cool. "Kaminski is a good tenant. I mean he's quiet and he pays the rent on time. He brings in the milk if it's out. But you've seen what he looks like. And yesterday I swear I saw him bringing in a gun. So I don't know."

"Shit!" Martin's thoughts leapt immediately to Gerard Butler movies, Eastern underworld drug bosses, and the Polish immigrants who had arrived seeking a better world only to find no jobs and no pot of gold at the end of the relocation rainbow. "Are you going to be all right?"

Billy laughed. "I'll be fine. If the police hassle me about him, I'll just ask him to leave. It's not like he's running some kind of bomb factory in my basement."

"I guess," Martin agreed, though he couldn't think of a nonsinister reason for the police to come barging in the door at this time in the morning. "Why don't you come back to the show with me? We've got spare kit; we can always use another Viking."

Billy ducked his head to hide his smile. It was a good face, now Martin could see it, with a strong nose and a pointed chin and cheekbones that seemed to combine hardness with elegance. But Billy spent half his time trying to conceal it, turning away, looking down. The face paint had drawn a confidence out of him he couldn't seem to muster without it. "My neighbour upstairs can't get around much. I can't leave her to handle this."

"Then d'you want me to stay?"

Bad idea. God, that would be a terrible idea, for the leader of a nascent society to abandon them on their very first show. Rolf would carry on without him, but he'd rightly be treated like a piece of scum if he ever turned up again.

The thought must have shown in his face because Billy shook his head and shoved him in the centre of the chest, edging him down the stone steps at the entrance of the house and out onto the pavement. A milk float was rattling past, and from the village church came the shattering sound of the bells striking seven o'clock.

Martin looked around. The haze was already beginning to lift, but the streets were still empty. No one was watching, no one to disapprove or see. So he reached up to slide his fingers into the hair at the back of Billy's neck and pull him down into a kiss. "You will call me, yeah?"

"I will."

When he let Billy go, the man's head remained bent, his gaze fixed on the ground, too downcast for Martin's liking. So he hooked a hand around Billy's chin, pushed his face back up, and got one fleeting glance from periwinkle-blue eyes for his trouble. They looked worried but amused. Billy's smile was obviously at least half-genuine.

"Good. Good, then." Again, Martin found himself wishing he'd not taken on this leadership role in Bretwalda. When he'd started reenacting, he could turn up in kit when he liked, laze about the civilian exhibit, do some whittling, fight in the daily battle, eat when he liked, go home when he liked, with nothing more worrying to transport than a shield and a spear.

How had he ever got to the stage where if he wasn't there the entire thing would fall apart? He'd picked up responsibility not because he wanted it, but just because other people had left it lying around. Now he didn't know how to put it back down. "I wish I could stay."

The awkwardness seemed to strike them both at the same time. They laughed, and with one final kiss Martin turned and strode off to his car. He saw Billy wait a long time on the front doorstep, watching as he drove away. One final wave as he turned the corner, and then he was back on the road, wishing for the first time ever that he could have more real life instead of more of the fake.

CHAPTER THIRTEEN

"Mr. Deng? Could I have a word?" The Head caught Martin as he unwisely left the staff room to visit the toilets. Monday morning had come with its usual culture shock, moving him out of the simple vivid world of the resurrected ninth century and into grey corridors and the smell of school lunches. There had been no email and no phone call from Billy, and Martin already had the feeling the week was going to be shit.

He followed the Head into her office with something of the trepidation the children must feel when they were summoned to account for themselves. At least he didn't have to stand in front of the Ikea desk, but was allowed to lower himself gently to the creaking, arthritic chair. The Head flipped open a green cardboard file.

God, this was serious then, if it was generating paperwork.

"Mr. Deng. Under normal circumstances the hobbies of a member of staff would be no concern of mine."

"Mm-hmm."

The Head took a handkerchief from her top pocket and wiped her hands on it. Then she drew open her desk drawer and brought out a bottle of perfume, which she sprayed on the linen. Raising it to her nose, she sniffed. "Are you aware that you stink?"

Martin stiffened on the fragile chair as his heart seemed to miss a beat. She couldn't say something like that, could she?

"The smoke, I mean." A hand gesture as if fanning the miasma away. "You smell of smoke."

"Yes. I'm sorry about that. It gets in the braids. It'll fade in a day or two."

"And you can't... wash them, or shave them off, or something?"

That was almost equally unbelievable. "I could shave all my hair off, yes. Have you considered asking Miss Timeon to do the same?"

The Head pulled her shoulders up as if bracing for a fight. "I wouldn't dream of it."

"Her extensions always smell like burnt plastic, which is a much worse smell than smoke. If she agrees to shave hers off, I'll do mine."

"Miss Timeon is a young lady. I would not dream of asking her. The cases are not the same." The Head twitched and shifted on her seat as though it were biting her, and Martin rather hoped that it was.

"Yeah, well, as far as I know, you can't tell me what to do with my hair either. Is that all?"

Under her polished silver hair, the Head had a droopy face, bags under her eyes, jowls to her collar, and a slack mouth that in a vanished youth might once have been sensuous. This closed and thinned on a flash of temper as she went rigid with disapproval.

"It is not. If you recall, you were warned on Friday that your hobby was taking up unacceptable amounts of your time. You were told to cut it back or face the consequences." She gave Martin a righteous look, as of someone enjoying their upper hand. "At which point you immediately booked unpaid leave for that very afternoon."

"I had one lesson. My class had just done extremely well on a history quiz, and I'd promised them a video that afternoon. I arranged for an alternate teacher to be there to switch the TV on and off and deal with any disruption. I didn't need to—"

Martin might have felt panicky if he had not still been in a state of disbelief and anger after the haircutting comment. As it was, he felt oddly cold and sharp and untouchable.

"My point stands," the Head interrupted. "You were given a warning which you immediately disregarded. You have exhibited frankly unacceptable behaviour in this interview and an unwillingness to make the slightest concession to this school's expectations. You have marking which should have been done and turned in over this weekend, but which has not been done. And I'm afraid we're going to have to let you go."

Martin's brain tripped over the words, stumbled. What?

Yes, to be fair, he'd expected a dressing down. He'd been angry, and he'd left early as a giant fuck-you to the establishment. He'd come in braced for another warning, still undecided about what to do with her last ultimatum, worried that the fact he was now in a gay relationship showed somehow, and semiresigned to going on teaching the things he needed to teach until someone took decisive action one way or another. But this? It was too soon. He wasn't prepared. He'd thought there'd be three strikes or something, a grace period over which he could look for another placement, or during which she might be forced by age and unpopularity to finally retire.

We're going to have to let you go. His mouth had dried and his throat withered shut. It wasn't meant to go this far. She hadn't even given him a chance to tell her to shove her Victorian attitude to his enriched history syllabus. If he was going to go, damn it, it should have been on his terms, as an act of principle. Not because of some stupid petty rules about haircuts and holidays.

He could take this to a tribunal. He could fight this. He could make them keep him on. They couldn't do this to him! He was a bloody good teacher. They wouldn't find another one better.

Like a bubble in a tar pit, the thought welled and popped. *You wanted more time. Now you have it.* It was not at all funny.

After the initial rush of fury and denial, second thoughts about the tribunal surfaced. It would be a lot of work and expense. Even if he won, he would become known throughout the district as difficult to work with. Litigious. More trouble than he was worth. It could spell the end of his teaching career. People might be sent to look into his lifestyle, and then who knew what slander might be dropped? Innocence was no defence against rabid parents who didn't want a queer teaching their darling boys. And he was no longer sure he even wanted to work in this place if it meant feeding the kids the kind of history that made them feel bad about themselves.

"Okay. Okay, fine." He forced the words out, still too annoyed to be properly devastated. "Effective as of . . . ?"

"You will of course be given a month's notice and pay. But frankly, Mr. Deng, I would rather you didn't work that month. It so happens that we have an applicant for the post who can begin tomorrow. So consider it something of a gift—a month's pay. No need to earn it."

He tried to think of a cutting parting remark, something pithy and pointed that she would remember for years, but nothing came. Eventually he second-guessed himself into thinking that would be unprofessional and unworthy of him anyway. The appropriate Viking response, to cleave the woman's skull and then boast about it in the assembly hall, was certainly less than helpful.

"Charlie will make sure you have the paperwork by the end of today."

"Yes, ma'am."

"I suggest you go and clear out your desk."

Denial and sympathy got him through the rest of the day. The other teachers responded with emergency cream cakes and hand-drawn cards. It wasn't until he had driven home and was putting his school mug on the drying rack beside his home mugs that the reaction truly hit.

Shit. He wandered empty-handed into the living room and stood amongst the detritus of his life, trying not to feel empty, even afraid. He was unemployed. With a mortgage he'd barely been able to afford as it was, in a region where there were more trained teachers than schools to employ them. He had microwave chips and a half jar of coffee in the house. The breakdown cover on his car was due.

It was Sheena's birthday in two weeks. He hadn't got her a present and couldn't now afford anything decent. Thinking about his father's reaction made him want to drink all the alcohol in the house in one go. There was a show coming up in a fortnight in Scotland, and no way he could afford the petrol to get there with the trailer containing all the society's camping equipment.

And Billy still hadn't called.

Martin stripped off his school clothes, putting them in the washing machine with a dose of powder and an added pang of failure. Then he had a long shower, with the radio turned up high, the hot water beating imaginary pains out of his neck and back. Clean and dressed in clothes he associated with leisure, he felt a little better. Still had a month of wages, after all. No need to starve quite yet. Something would come up. He would make something turn up.

Bretwalda's leftover food was stacked on his kitchen counter. As he wondered what he could make with leeks, eggs, and an excessive amount of wholemeal bread, the phone jangled from its receiver in the hallway.

Thank God. His spirits lifted at the thought of speaking to Billy, whose bass voice was softened with that little country burr of his. If he was feeling well enough to ring, he might be well enough to laugh, and Martin was eager to hear that. Maybe he'd even be up to a little light phone sex, shy and awkward and cute as fuck.

"Martin Deng." He sandwiched the phone between his ear and shoulder, almost smiling, and went back into the kitchen. Leek omelette and toast? Some kind of cheesy, eggy bread?

"Martin, it's your father."

Martin put down the loaf abruptly, his hand rising to hold the receiver properly. He closed his eyes for the count of three, shoved back bad news and disappointment together. "Hi, Dad."

"Your mother asked me to remind you that it's Sheena's birthday coming up on the first of June."

He was twenty-six. He was twenty-six years old, damn it. He should not have this knee-jerk defensiveness, this prickly assumption that he was being disrespected. "I know that, Dad. Sheena's the one who forgets birthdays. I never do."

"Well, we're having a party for her at our house. Are you coming up to London to see us all?"

That was the Scottish show. Up in Kirkcudbright, where it never stopped raining. Martin eased himself up onto the tall stool by the breakfast bar, feeling like he needed to be sitting down for this.

"I can't. I'm in Scotland that weekend."

The low growl of displeasure. "It's your sister. Your family. Once a year and you can't be here?"

"I already told Sheena, and she said it was fine." He picked at the laminate edge of the tabletop, feeling small and guilty and conscious of his own anger because of it. Sheena had told him that she didn't actually want a party. If she had her choice, she'd said, she would have had a spa weekend on her own, where she could unwind from too much exposure to people, not a gathering of the clans that would leave her exhausted and down. But Martin knew he couldn't say that, couldn't criticise, could only take what was dished out to him, not give it back.

"Are you ashamed of us?" His father's voice was accusing, stern. He thought he was supposed to be able to read love in it, but he could only hear the rebuke.

"No, it's not that." *It's that you are ashamed of me.* "I just. I can't afford to come to London, to buy the kind of suit I'd have to wear at whatever hotel you're having this at. I can't . . ."

I can't afford food, rent. The thought of money was a choke chain around his neck.

"If you put a little work in, you could be head of that school. You should look the part at least. People notice these things. Success comes to the successful."

He didn't want to say it, wanted his father to stop being interested in his life. It would be absolutely ideal if they were never to speak again. "I lost my job, Dad."

"What!" The tone of the conversation plummeted. "Oh, Martin. Why? Why are you like this, when we tried so hard to educate you and teach you the value of hard work? Why must you always—"

"Dad, please don't." Martin bowed his head into his hands. *And this, this is the reason I won't be coming to London. This is the reason I don't visit. This is the reason I don't call. Because when I do, you make me feel like shit.* "I don't want to talk about this right now. I'm looking at other schools. There are always more kids to be taught. It's not the end of the world."

"Martin." Serious, stern. Martin knew this tone of voice. *Oh, here we go*, he thought, *"When I was in Khartoum . . ."*

"You say it's not the end of the world, but it could be. When I was little, our neighbours heard about the civil war and they said, 'We are peaceable people here. What has this got to do with us?' But your grandfather sold his cattle, and when the soldiers came for our neighbours, he got us out."

"Yes, Dad," Martin said, trying to massage the ache out of his scalp. Repetition had worn away his sympathy a long time ago.

"'We are safe here,' they said, when we were in the Nuba Mountains, with all the other refugees. 'Wars do not come here.' But famine came instead. If your grandfather had not worked hard, saved money, we would not have been able to leave again and find work in Khartoum. If we had not been wealthy, *respectable* people, I would not have been able to study medicine and become a doctor, and get away to this place where war has not yet come."

"I know that, Dad."

"Don't think you are safe," his father pressed. Martin knew, intellectually, that this was the sound of concern for him, a parent's fear for his child's future. It just didn't feel like that. It felt like being slowly squashed by an enormous stone.

"In Sudan, the Nuer would kill you because you were Dinka. Here that at least doesn't matter, but they see that you are black and that puts you one step away from safety. Do not make the mistake of being poor as well."

"I didn't lose my job out of spite, Dad. I didn't mean to! I'm going to find another; it's no big deal."

A put-upon silence, but Martin must have sounded at the end of his tether because his father let it go. "At least tell me you're seeing a nice girl. Someone with prospects and connections, who can help you. If you can't be a doctor, perhaps you can marry one."

Yes, well if there had ever been a time he *could* face telling his father he was gay, this was not it. One deviation from respectability at a time. He slid his thumbnail under the laminate, peeled a strip off, and then wished he hadn't. Did he say anything at all about Billy? Did he say, *Well, I am seeing someone, but I'm not going to tell you anything about them for fear you'll figure out he's a man*?

No, of course he didn't. "I think maybe I should concentrate on the job right now, don't you? I'll worry about courting when I'm settled again."

His father heaved a deep, sepulchral sigh, as if Martin's very existence sucked all the life out of him. "I did think you would visit for your sister's sake."

Martin dug his thumb into the table again, and a sliver of veneer poked up under his nail like a poisoned thorn. He clasped it tight, bent over it, struggling not to swear, and earnestly tried to shut the conversation down. "Yes, well, I'll come when I've got a new job and I can afford to travel. Some time in the autumn half term, I hope. Give my love to Mum."

"She's wondering when she's going to get grandchildren." He could hear the narrowed eyes, even over the phone.

"Dad, I'm twenty-six. There's plenty of time yet. I'll... um, I'll call you when I've got some news. Okay?"

Another sigh, and an inaudible grumble. *Fuck off*, Martin thought, feeling so wound up he was almost ready to say it out loud.

"Very well. I'm sure Sheena is quite used to the disappointment by now. Take care of yourself, Martin. And do try to do better in future."

He rolled his eyes to the ceiling, but it did nothing to help alleviate the desire to take an axe to his kitchen cupboards. "I will, Dad. Speak to you later."

"Good-bye."

Fucker. Fucking bastard. Martin made scrambled egg on toast with shaking hands and ate it viciously, washing it down with all the beer he had left from the weekend. The alcohol gradually took the edge off his anger and let the hurt out instead. He went to bed miserable, not sure if it made it better or worse to reflect that this must be what Billy felt like most of the time.

No wonder he hadn't called.

CHAPTER FOURTEEN

The thought of Billy was what got him out of bed in the morning. With no need to go to work, he might have just rolled over and snoozed until noon, wallowing in surly self-pity, if he had not wanted to see whether Billy had sent him an email.

He hadn't. But now he was in front of the computer, Martin felt obliged to check all the job and educational websites. He made a list of vacancies for which he could apply, updated his CV, and turned in a half-dozen applications by email, printing out copies for those stone-age institutions that still did their business by paper.

It felt better to be doing things. He felt better about himself once he was up and dressed, showered, with clean teeth and breakfast inside him. The ball of nerves and panic that had made its home in his heart at the thought of an extended period out of work was made manageable by the distraction.

After lunch—more toast—he trekked down to the post office and sent out his printed applications. Thought about going to the job centre to register as unemployed and then shoved the thought away. There was still time to fix this. It would be okay. He would only admit defeat, crawl to the government for help, next month if he hadn't got a new job once his month's notice was up.

But he would sign on, ask for housing benefit and jobseeker's allowance, rather than give up the flat and skulk back to his parents' house. It was okay. It would not come to that.

Returning home, he found that Billy had still not called. One more worry to swallow down. He pinched the top of his nose, allowed himself to bow his head for a moment under the weight, and then straightened up and gave his living room a speculative glance.

How to get the money to buy petrol to transport Bretwalda's kit to Scotland?

A warp-weighted loom leaned against his bookshelf, but he couldn't bear the thought of parting with that. He had more tablet weave than he strictly needed. He could maybe sell the shaving horse and then make himself a new one with some of the logs from the garden. And that wool...

Oh, that wool!

Martin pulled the fabric from behind the sofa and laid it ceremonially in the small expanse of free floor space. He rolled a foot of fabric out and gazed at it in reverence, reaching to rub a corner between his thumb and fingers.

Hand spun on drop spindles, hand dyed using nothing more than native dye plants and cauldrons, hand woven on the warp-weighted loom, it was a masterpiece of craft. It was as close to the real thing as humanly possible. All the threads were fine and even, the subtly speckled pattern of the orangy-red colour caused by the wool being dyed before it was spun—drying and lightening slightly on the outside of the hank, giving a flecked appearance when it was spun. The diamond-patterned weave added a further layer of complexity and texture.

It had cost him ridiculous amounts of money, and even so, he'd known he wasn't paying enough for the amount of work that went into it. He'd been keeping it to make a cloak, a cloak that would make him the envy of every reenactor in the world. He'd just kept putting it off because it had seemed like too much of a blasphemy to cut the stuff.

Telling himself a blatant lie—that it was only a thing, that it wasn't important—he phoned the guy who had most coveted it, the guy who thought nothing of dropping a couple of hundred pounds on a new sword, or a gold-studded belt or a replica Sutton Hoo helmet. His old group leader.

"Hi Brian. I'm clearing out some stuff. I wondered if you were still interested..."

The rest of the day passed without word from Billy. Martin told himself that he shouldn't expect the guy to be prompt with his responses. Sheena was forever sending out belated birthday cards, belated Christmas cards, because she'd gotten to it as soon as she could, but that hadn't been soon enough.

Martin was used to waiting for signs of love, concern, interest, until the other person was well enough to give them. But of course he'd grown up with Sheena and was confident of her regard. Billy might not be calling because he didn't want to. He might have decided Martin's impulsive visit was a bit stalkery, might be resenting the fact that Martin had pushed things faster than he was ready to go.

If so, getting in contact with the guy from his end would only be compounding the problem.

He rolled out of bed on Wednesday more reluctantly, because Brian was coming, and told himself that if Billy hadn't called by the end of the week he would ...

Give up?

No, he would phone, give it one last shot. It wasn't fair to expect Billy to do all the running if the guy had difficulties in doing more than his normal routine. He just hoped it wouldn't come to that.

Brian arrived at half two, having taken the afternoon off from his job as an IT tech in some small components firm in Trowbridge. His knock on the door brought back memories, and it was briefly pleasurable to see him come in, moving with the deceptive shamble of a silver-backed gorilla through Martin's flat. The hall seemed too small for him. Even without armour on, the guy was impressive, his layer of fat and his substantial beer belly carried lightly on a bulk of muscle.

Brian was somewhere around sixty years of age, his white hair pulled back into a ponytail at the base of his neck. His moustache was waxed into points and his beard plaited and finished off with a red glass bead. Still a biker, with engine grease under his fingernails and interlaced tattoos up his gnarled arms.

"Well." He looked about with curiosity and, Martin thought, condescension. Not enough engine parts on the floor, maybe. "Long time no see, Ametel. How you been doing out there on your own?"

Martin smiled and flourished a mug. It was nice that Brian had remembered his Merotic name—the name by which his reenactment character was known. Brian himself was Ketil when he was in character, which Martin secretly found hilarious.

"Not too bad," he said, as was only right. No one asked these things because they actually wanted to know. "Cup of tea?"

"Dying for one."

Martin ducked into the kitchen, leaving Brian at large in the living room on his own. "What about you?" he called through the open door.

"Oh, good. We've had a good season for recruiting. Got five newbies at once, if you believe it, from a show we did for the university."

Martin made a mental note to try to book some events for Bretwalda where concentrations of young people hung out. Give it a couple of months and try Trowbridge to see if anyone had dropped out of their Summer Spectacular. Maybe Trowchester Academy would be interested in something for their summer ball? He wasn't convinced by the mental picture of a bunch of drunk students in their party frocks watching a fake battle, but they could do *something*, surely?

"Course, a couple of them were queer as fuck." Brian laughed, good-humouredly, inviting Martin to share the joke. Martin's fingers clenched hard on the teaspoon with which he was adding three spoons of sugar to Brian's tea, bending the metal with his grip.

"Seriously, you should have seen them." Brian chuckled again. "Raging poofters, they were."

Martin sidled into his own living room like he was unwelcome, put down the mugs of tea on one of the many wooden stools that littered the floor. The same feelings of guilt and rage, inadequacy and shame that he had when he spoke to his father were curling through him again. He felt like a toilet that had just been flushed—forced to swallow down filth. He wanted to spit it all out but couldn't quite find certainty and footing enough.

Brian cocked a hip and made like a teapot, warbling in a falsetto voice, "Ooh, everything's so dirty. I'm getting soot on my nice shoes."

You'll get a knee in your fucking balls if you carry on like that, Martin thought, but to his shame he said nothing. Just swallowed.

"Worse than the women," Brian noted with satisfaction. "Course they didn't last."

Martin gritted his teeth and thought again about recruitment. He could get the names, offer a refuge. "You threw them out?"

"Course not! What d'you think we are?" Brian was honestly indignant, as though the thought that anyone could possibly think he was homophobic was downright insulting. "They just had no sense of humour, po-faced bastards. They couldn't take a joke. And you know what the society's like—you gotta have a sense of humour, right? You can't be too much of a special snowflake about this stuff."

"Yeah," Martin agreed, sinking his face into his cup and despising himself for not saying anything.

Damn it, he'd left the society to get away from this, and while Brian was proving what a good move that had been, Kayleigh's "this brooch is so gay" comment had rubbed him exactly the same way. He should say something. He should not let this go past him unchallenged. He should get into the habit of knocking it back so it didn't take root in his own society and end up driving him out. Except what if it already was there, quieter, more insidious, and he wouldn't know until too late—until he'd told them and been rejected?

"You remember Dave Bryson?" he managed.

"Biscop Benedict." Brian looked about for the biscuits, and Martin dived back into the kitchen to bring them. "Yeah, good bloke."

"He was gay, you know."

A moment's feeling of tiny triumph because he had set his trap well, because he had at least got Brian to acknowledge that a gay guy could be a good bloke. But then Brian dunked a digestive in his tea and raised his eyebrows. "You don't say? Well, that explains a lot."

"Sorry?"

"Well, you know. Not fighting. Poncing about in purple silk. All that incense and singing. Always thought he was a bit nancy. I don't know why I'm surprised. He kept that quiet, though. I wonder why?"

"Yeah, who knows." Martin pinched his protest back behind his thinned lips and decided he'd had about enough of this. "So, that wool."

He flicked the roll open to show that the colour hadn't faded. "They said it was pretty colour fast, but I've kept it in the dark anyway, so it's... it's pristine."

Brian slid off the sofa onto one knee next to the bolt and examined the thread count with a discerning eye. "Your new society having problems, then? If you have to sell this?"

"It's not the society," Martin snapped. "I've lost my job. The fee from our next show will cover the society's bills, but only after we've done it and been paid. So I need some other means to drum up the petrol money beforehand. And this . . . well, I'd never dare wear it anyway. I got it for three hundred and fifty quid, so I'll give it to you for three hundred."

Unrolling the bolt, Brian slung the fabric over one shoulder and admired himself in the black reflective surface of the TV, pulling it in at the waist to look like a tunic, checking the way it draped, the way the skirt flared out when he moved.

Martin watched, in two minds. The part of him that was a ninth-century Viking noted regretfully how awesome the fabric looked—how the folds fell exactly as they were depicted on the carvings and the manuscripts of the time. The part of him that was a modern man reflected caustically on how "gay" it was of Brian to be admiring his pretty dress in the mirror.

"It's a deal," Brian said. They exchanged a handshake and then money, counted out in twenty-pound notes into Martin's hand. He and Martin rolled the material back into the old curtain in which Martin had been keeping it dark and safe and under wraps.

Brian picked it up and tucked it under his arm. "Listen, kiddo. If you get fed up with all the work, you know you'd be welcomed back. You and all the splitters who went with you. I was sad to see you all go, no kidding."

That was enough to give Martin an ache in his chest because yes, there had been good times, full of the rough and ready camaraderie that came from being the toughest, the most kick-ass, the most dangerous, the all-round-best society in the country.

But he couldn't say he was sad to go because if he did, Brian would ask him why he had felt the need to split in the first place, and he'd rather get out of it with the man's respect, even if it was fake, contingent on Martin being something he wasn't.

I'm one of those poofters myself. He could almost feel the words behind his teeth, filling his mouth like saliva. *All this time you've been thinking I was one of the lads, and actually I was gay. And no, I don't have a sense of humour, because I don't find it funny to be mocked.*

But what good would it do to tell Brian now, when he would probably never seen the man again? He swallowed the spit. "We're doing okay," he said instead, walking his guest out to the car. "But yeah, if it doesn't work out, then thanks."

Why did you do that? he asked himself as he watched the car drive away. *You hate people falsifying the past. Why do you falsify your present?*

Because I'm not putting one more thing in the way of getting a new job. I'm not giving Dad one more thing to complain about. I'm not making it even harder to get anyone to do anything I say in Bretwalda, and I'm not . . . I'm just not ready.

Feeling tired and vaguely unclean, he switched the computer back on, intending to check whether anyone had offered him an interview. No one had, but his despondency was interrupted when his email programme flashed up a window that made him catch his breath, telling him he had new messages.

It flickered out before he could be sure what he'd seen. Something about morris, from an address he didn't recognise. Trying not to get his hopes up, he clicked through to his emails and yes, there was one labelled "history of morris" that he could not imagine would have come from anyone other than Billy.

He opened it up with an easing around his heart. One good thing in a shit day.

Thought you'd like to see this, the message said, with a link to a website that took the origins of morris dancing back to the fifteenth century, and showed him pictures of guys in doublets with sleeves that grazed the ground. A medieval lady stood like a judging queen in the centre of a ring of dancers, all of whom were trying to impress her with their capering.

It was very odd. Billy had included a quote from a seventeenth-century Puritan who obviously regarded the dance as a highway to hell. *"It hath been tould that your morice dauncers have daunced naked in nettes: what greater entisement unto naughtines could have been devised?"* And despite everything that had gone wrong today, that was so bizarre it made Martin laugh out loud.

He'd thought that perhaps the Griffins were fooling themselves when they talked about the history behind what they did. He was impressed to find they had evidence, some kind of rigour. This brush with the sheer strangeness of humanity had the same texture as the experience he had when reading ibn Fadlan, seeing the Vikings from the inside.

Encountering the minds of people from history was like encountering aliens. Funny and bizarre, unsettling and uncomfortable, sometimes even repellent. But you always returned from it with a refreshed perspective, so that just for a little while, before habit kicked back in, you could see your own world with a stranger's eyes, and all the things that were normally invisible showed up like cancer cells tagged with radiant dye.

It put his problems into perspective, for a while at least.

There's a session at the King's Arms tonight, Billy's email finished. *I wondered if you'd like to come. But then I thought you're hardly going to want to drive an hour here and then have to drive an hour back in time for work in the morning. So maybe you could come at the weekend?*

Martin thought about breakdown cover and the cost of petrol, and then he thought, *Oh, what the hell.* He had just come into three hundred pounds, and he might as well enjoy the advantages of joblessness, such as they were.

He put another sheaf of copies of his printed CV into envelopes and dropped them in the postbox on the way out, phoning Billy this time to let him know he was on his way.

CHAPTER
FIFTEEN

Martin had not been sure what "a session" was, but had assumed it would be something to do with morris dancing. As he pushed through throngs of people, young and old, filling the pub's large back room, he could see there wasn't floor space enough for that.

The room was packed so close with tables it was hardly possible to edge past them to the bar. He ordered two pints of Theakston's Old Peculier and two packets of crisps as he watched the crowd squeeze themselves onto chairs and begin to assemble equipment out of the many rigid black cases they had brought with them.

Outside the windows of the room, weeping willows trailed against the brickwork, and he could see the waters of the Arborough Drain surge like a tide towards the sea. Although he only lived an hour's drive away, he had the strong impression that stepping into the marshlands was stepping back in time by at least twenty or thirty years. It gave him an unexpected sympathy with the Griffins' view that reenactment was theatre—dressing up, playing let's pretend—whereas what they did was a continuance of the past. Theirs was a live tradition, his a dead one.

"You all right there?" Billy asked. Tonight he was smiling. Something loose and relaxed about his long limbs indicated he was having a good day. They stood together next to the bar and Martin noticed that the flow of people streamed straight past Billy. He was constantly having to move aside as folk went through him as though he weren't there.

Martin edged a barstool out for him with his foot, so that Billy could get out of the way properly. They hopped up together and Billy opened his own black case, taking out a violin.

The close-packed tables in the centre of the room were now covered in beer glasses, wicker baskets containing complimentary chips, and more musical instruments than Martin had ever seen in his life. Things were being screwed onto other things, folded out, clipped together, or otherwise assembled.

There was a sense of anticipation and an odd discomfort, as though something momentous was about to happen and no one could be entirely sure it would turn out well. Billy smiled at Martin and screwed a wood-and-leather ledge onto the underside of his violin, swinging the instrument round to check that the rest sat comfortably on his shoulder. "You've not been to one of these before?"

"No." Martin felt a little wild-eyed, like an anthropologist coming across an entirely new culture. "Is it okay to be here if you don't play anything?"

"Oh yes. Everyone loves a listener."

A clink of a coin on a beer glass called the room to order. Everyone quieted as a frumpy, middle-aged woman with some kind of squeeze-box strapped to her chest got up to welcome them and suggest a first tune. She sat down, and Martin braced himself for the grown-up equivalent of school music lessons. When Mrs. Palmer at *that place where he didn't work anymore* left her classroom doors open in the summer, the sound of the school orchestra pervaded the whole building like the smell of cabbage. All the squeaking recorders and sawing violins and bassoons like the horns of passing taxis.

But this . . . They did take a while to start up. One guy played something plaintive and soft on the Irish pipes, the sound like whisky—misty, oak flavoured, eerie. Then Billy joined in. The purer notes of the fiddle intertwined with the rasp of the pipe, and although he was playing the same tune, the effect was of more than double the complexity. As each new instrument joined in, adding its unique voice, a whole was created more powerful than the combination, until it seemed that they'd opened a portal and something alive had entered the room, independent of them all.

It gave Martin the shivers. He'd always thought of music as being the purview of specialists. You got bands who were intensively managed and packaged by the industry, or you got classical musicians, who were intensively managed and packaged by their orchestras. Either way, music was like everything else in the modern world—too sophisticated to be done by ordinary people. Another form of self-expression, of creativity, taken out of the hands of the common man and given over entirely to trained professionals.

Clearly he couldn't have been more wrong. Here it was, music in the hands of ordinary people, more powerful, more beautiful and *stranger* than he had suspected.

Being outside it, watching Billy become part of this collective creature, made him feel left behind. Beautiful though it was, Billy was wrong: this was not a spectator sport. This was not a place for anyone who was not involved.

He glanced along the bar, to where other partners of musicians sat with their empty hands curved around their beer glasses, looking as enraptured and as disenfranchised as he felt.

Billy was swaying on his stool, knee bouncing as he tapped his foot, his body wanting to dance to the music he was making. Martin's thoughts connected this with reenactment and history and teaching, as he wondered what he could do to share this with others. Did the Vikings dance? Did they make music? What would it have looked like? Sounded like? Why had he never thought about it before?

"You look very thoughtful," said Billy in a lowered voice, while a lone guitarist played something Spanish and complicated that clearly no one else knew well enough to join in with. Those blue eyes of his were shining and sure of themselves, his face aglow. Martin was three pints in by then, hazy and content, and it seemed right that Billy should be backed by a musical theme of aching sweetness. Look what he had inside him—all this music, all this grace. What a magical creature he was.

"Thank you," he said, feeling something close to awe that Billy had reached out to him. It was as though he had hunkered down and waited, and a spotted fawn had trusted him enough to tiptoe out of the forest and nuzzle at his hand. Not that he could *say* that, of course. "For inviting me. It feels like a real honour. I didn't even know this kind of thing existed before. I bet the Vikings did something similar, in the evenings in their mead halls. I wonder what that would have been like."

Billy laughed, but didn't taunt him for his monomania. That too was a balm to Martin's soul. But then Billy presumably also knew what it was like to live for one's hobby.

"What kind of instruments did they have in those days?"

"I don't know." Martin's curiosity gave a bound of interest and completed his recovery. Having something to research was also a good reason to get up in the morning. "But I can find out."

When the session wound down at midnight, they walked back to Billy's house. All around the village, fields planted with oilseed rape were blossoming, and the warm night air was heavy with its scent.

"What happened with your tenant?" Martin asked, as they passed the heavily locked flat on their way upstairs. "Did they arrest him?"

Billy shrugged one shoulder and put his violin case down to unlock his own door. "I don't know what happened. The police stayed awhile and then they went. Kaminski's still there." He looked uncertain and a little tired as he gestured for Martin to go in, snapping the lights on and following. "They would have arrested him if there was something seriously wrong, wouldn't they? I mean, if he was making bombs down there or something."

"You'd hope so." Martin took the case from Billy and put it down carefully in a corner before pulling him into a long, filthy kiss. The question of the mobster lodger eased its way towards irrelevance as he felt Billy's mind turn from music towards his other senses. "Though they might have arrested him and then released him on bail."

"I should ask him about it." Billy hooked his fingers through Martin's belt loops and walked backwards, hauling him into the bedroom. Martin struggled a little just for the fun of it, grinning all over his face.

"I really don't think that's a good idea," he managed nevertheless. "Do not piss off the man with the guns."

Billy laughed, as though he thought Martin was making a joke, and Martin paused in the act of peeling him out of his shirt to shake him by both biceps. "Listen, I mean that, okay? Even if he's not some kind of Russian mafia thug, he's pretty clearly aggressive and paranoid and if he's in possession of live ammunition too, then leave him alone, okay? Let the police deal with it."

Billy flinched and turned his face aside, and Martin remembered belatedly that his springbok was fragile. Browbeating was probably too much for him to handle. He curved a hand around Billy's cheek and brought his face back, kissed the moment of rejection away.

"I can see I'm going to have to give you something else to think about," he said, drawing them both down to a bed that was beginning to feel familiar. *Just like you've done for me today.* Because it was remarkable how much better he felt now he was worrying about Billy than when all he had to worry about was himself.

Next morning, Martin woke slowly to the consciousness of contentment. Having Billy's slender form in his arms felt right. It felt complete. Even the ceiling of Billy's flat, with its off-white paint and cracked plaster, seemed friendlier than his own. They ate breakfast together in a pocket of quiet as soothing as ointment on a graze.

"I lost my job," he confessed, as Billy looked at the clock for the third time. "I don't have to rush off."

He half expected Billy to sneer, had his defences up, just in case, but all Billy did was to get up to put the kettle on again, and say, "Oh, I'm sorry," as if he meant it. "But I'm sure you'll get another one soon. I don't know where they'd find another history teacher who cares as much as you."

Martin sipped his tea, closed his eyes, and felt solid again. *You see?* he said to his father in the safety of his own mind. *That's the kind of reaction I was hoping for. One that made me feel that at least someone believes in me.*

Billy replenished the big blue teapot with more hot water and another tea bag. He'd sucked his lower lip into his mouth as if he were chewing it, thinking something over. Martin had a hunch that he was wondering whether to suggest that Martin should just stay, then. Stay and look for a job closer to Billy's house. In a twist of unsuspected yearning, he thought he would like that, actually. But in the end, Billy didn't say it and Martin felt it was too early in the relationship for him to ask.

"Can I Skype you this evening?" he said instead. "This village seems like a really fast-paced place. I need to keep in touch with the news."

Billy coloured up. He ducked his head, but Martin had already caught the smile and been charmed. "I don't . . . I'm not very good at chatting."

"That's okay. I'm not great at it either, to tell the truth. But we could have the window open while we do other stuff, and it would be like we were together. I wouldn't want to go to bed without wishing you goodnight."

Tipping his now-red face into his hands, Billy chuckled. "Well, if you really would like that."

"I really would."

Over the next few weeks, Martin sat through five job interviews, doing his best to be charming, professional, interesting, personable, trustworthy, and dynamic. The rest of the time he staved off his feelings of despair and inadequacy by researching ancient dance and music along with Billy. They emailed almost constantly, phoned two or three times a day, and Martin found himself spending the whole day just waiting for Billy to get on Skype so he could see his pixelated face. Their Skype sessions slowly expanded from five minutes before bedtime to the whole evening. Skimping on his meals to save up for petrol so that they could spend the weekends together, Martin felt hopeful, blessed, job situation notwithstanding.

The Scottish show went well. Even the rain stopped after the first day, letting him pack everything away dry. He enjoyed it more for not being exhausted from work, but he didn't like being so far away from Billy. When he cut short time spent around the fire in the evenings so that he could spend it just chatting to Billy instead over the phone, it began to really dawn on him that he had it bad.

Edith had an Anglo-Saxon hearpe, which she had bought in a flush of love and enthusiasm and had never learned to play, chiefly because nobody knew how it had been played in the first place. They had no music for it, and no one was available to teach her. In his new enthusiasm for all things musical, Martin borrowed the instrument from her and took it home with him. He'd hoped to find at least a couple of offers for job interviews in his email folder when he got back, if not an actual offer of employment, but he got none. New relationships and . . . love . . . aside, that was ever so slightly crushing.

So he fled from it by taking the hearpe to show to Billy before the engine of his car had barely had time to get cool.

"It's a kind of lyre?" Billy asked, turning it in his hands with the practical reverence of a musician. Edith had handled it as if it would bite; she was always very timid. Billy held it the way he held his violin, with just the right pressure for the thin wood of its sounding board. Confident but gentle, sure as the way in which he handled Martin. Once he had thought of the comparison, Martin had to grin. Billy touched him like a musical instrument—like a thing that gave joy.

"The Saxons called it a harp," he said, noticing that the depth of the instrument, which had always seemed ridiculously slim, was not actually much less than that of a violin. "Manuscripts show that it's plucked or strummed with one hand, while the other hand comes through the hole there at the top and blocks off the strings to make chords."

Manuscripts showed King David, from the Bible, holding the thing upright, the bottom of the body cradled in his lap, the thin curved arch of the top against his chest. Billy, however, positioned it like a guitar, sideways across his knees. He fiddled with the chords and the tuning for a while, and then launched into a rendition of "All You Need Is Love," with a strummed accompaniment.

"You know what?" Ruefully, Martin stirred the pan of spaghetti they had put on for their dinner. "Just about everyone in the society has tried to play that thing, and failed. I don't know why we never thought of giving it to an actual musician before. None of us are, you see."

"It's hard to play a musical instrument that nobody knows how to play, particularly if you've never played any other instrument in your life." Billy had now angled the top of the harp up to meet his chin, was curled over it, as if it and he were whispering secrets to each other. Martin thought perhaps they were.

"Do you like it? As a form of instrument it lasted for a very long time. Thousands of years. Things like that have been found in the pyramids. And then it reaches the year one thousand and disappears utterly, never to be seen again. It seems a shame, you know, that something so ancient should die out so completely."

"I do like it." Billy gave a twisted smile, as though he knew what obsolescence felt like. "There's no doubt it's limited, but then so is a single-row melodeon. It doesn't mean it's a bad instrument; it just means you have to pick the right music. Did you find any?"

"I did." Martin offered him the printouts of the very few tunes he had found from the ninth century. "What do you think?"

Billy looked through them, set the one called *The Wanderer* on top of the pile, and began to half pluck, half strum the notes, punctuating them with taps on the soundboard that made the lyre resonate like a drum. Already it sounded more like music to Martin than anything he'd heard a member of the society play.

"Can you get me any more of these? I know a couple of guitarists who could pick them up easily enough."

Martin sighed. "This is the only one in the society, and I can't afford to buy any more at the moment. The group is having to sub me for petrol as it is." He thought about the session they had attended—the violin and the pipes together, the very different instruments complementing each other. "But I can get hold of a bone whistle, a set of Jorvik panpipes, a kantele, and plenty of finger cymbals, if you can find anyone to play them."

Billy beamed up at him from his seat by the kitchen table. "Christine plays the whistle, bone or otherwise. Matt plays the harmonica, so he'd probably be at home with the panpipes. And I bet Annette, our fiddler, could adapt to the kantele, particularly if she was allowed to bow it. What about dancers, though? The Griffins are generally up for anything, but I don't see your hard men of the Dark Ages being keen to try experimental dance."

Martin thought about Rolf in his oily gambeson that reeked of pig fat, the world's largest sword hanging from one side of his belt and the world's largest axe on the other. Rolf in full chain mail, learning to caper. "Yes," he agreed, quailing inside a little at the memory of Brian's comments about the biscop—what all right-minded men would think of dancing when you could be fighting. "Rolf might think it was a bit girly."

Billy flourished his fork disapprovingly, but he laughed. "He doesn't want to say that around us. Graham'd be insulted anyone thought dancing wasn't manly, and Margery'd be insulted anyone thought 'girly' was a bad thing. But speaking of the Griffins, most of them will be down the pub this evening. Do you want to come?"

Martin would have been happy to spend this evening as he had most other evenings in Billy's presence, curled up together on the sofa, watching the History Channel or the occasional cooking programme or movie, but the idea that Billy was beginning to integrate him into the rest of his life gave him such a buzz of proud joy that he didn't hesitate to say yes. So they flung on light jackets, and on a whim Martin packed up the hearpe in its sheepskin case and brought it too.

It was a warm Friday night in June, and sunlight still slanted past the beeches that bordered the village green. The Griffins were already there when they arrived, sitting outside the pub at a couple of rough picnic tables shaded by green and white umbrellas. It somehow had not occurred to Martin that they would remember him, but when they did he kicked himself mentally and all his inner parts clenched up cold as he realized they might figure it out.

"Martin!" Annette shuffled up and indicated the bench next to her. Out of her greatcoat and veil, she was a slim woman in her forties, with dark-brown hair speckled with silver strands. Sallow skinned, she wore no makeup at all and had a thin, pointed nose that put him in mind of a Concorde. "What a pleasant surprise. I didn't know you'd kept in touch."

"We've been—" said Billy, and Martin was so terrified he was going to say "going out" that he jumped in and shut Billy down hard.

"We thought it would be fun to try to reconstruct Viking music and dance. Maybe get a demonstration together for one of the shows this year."

Billy's smile went out like a snuffed candle, and he felt dreadful about that, but he couldn't . . . He reached out and squeezed Billy's knee reassuringly under the cover of the table. Billy gave him a disappointed look, but then sighed, remembering, perhaps, their conversation at the show where they had met, agreeing to let it slide for now.

He went inside to buy a round of drinks in apology, and when he came back carrying a tray of clinking pint glasses, he found Billy explaining the harp to Annette.

She took her pint with a nod of thanks and a smile. "I was just saying, do you know the 'Abbots Bromley Horn Dance'?"

"I . . . uh." He sank down on the bench next to Billy. Billy's shoulders were relaxed again and his face smooth and engaged. Martin's consciousness of how terrible a person he was ebbed away enough for him to appreciate the warm summer evening, the windmill behind the Georgian houses across the empty road, and the cascades of flowers from all the pub's window boxes. "I don't know anything about dancing at all."

"We could use—" Billy began, and Matt cut him off as though he had not spoken at all.

"It should be well up your street. It's been danced every year in an unbroken tradition in Abbots Bromley since before records began."

"It's been my experience," Martin suggested—carefully, because he didn't know how Matt would take to his claiming any kind of intellectual equality—"that records don't tend to begin until the fifteenth or sixteenth century. Which would still make it too modern for us."

"Ah, but the thing is," Annette jumped in while Matt fiddled with his phone, "the dance is done with each dancer carrying a rack of antlers, which are stored in the church for the rest of the year, and someone, some anthropologist, or the like, dated the antlers with that radiocarbon dating thing."

"Oh yes, I heard about that," said Billy eagerly. "They were—"

"A thousand years old!" Matt finished, triumphantly holding out his phone.

They leaned together over its square surface, Martin with a hand on Billy's shoulder, ostensibly for balance, actually intended to reassure him that he was there, that he saw and heard Billy just fine, and he was sorry about the crassness of everyone else.

The sun made the little figures on the phone hard to pick out, but the tune rose from it as faint and melancholy as the smell of the trailing verbena above his head.

"I bet I could get something similar to that." Annette tucked the hearpe into her body and plucked an approximation of the haunting melody. It sounded even eerier under her hands.

"Well it's an easy enough dance." Matt looked up at his onlookers. "Let's try it."

Billy, Matt, redheaded Graham, and the white-haired Boy all perked up at the suggestion. "Colin's inside at the bar," said the Boy. "I'll get him. But that's still only five."

Billy nudged Martin with his knee, and Martin acknowledged that he had a lot to do to make it up to his springbok. He cleared his throat. "Well, if it's new to you too, I'll have less of a disadvantage. How about teaching me?"

The dance began simply enough. The six of them lined up in two lines of three, came together to meet in the centre, heads bowed as though they were stags clashing their antlers. Then a do-si-do manoeuvre he recognised from supervising some of McKay's country dance lessons. But then the set burst apart, turning first into a spiral and then a procession, and that was mind-bogglingly tricky to work out.

By the time the light was leaving the sky, they had it cracked. They danced it through once completely, while the occasional passing car slowed so the drivers could get a proper eyeful. It was probably the most English thing Martin had ever done—morris dancing on the village green in front of the pub, while the drinkers who had come out from the bar to watch heckled them good-humouredly, and the ducks on the village pond quacked out of time with the thin fragile music of the harp.

He sat down again exhilarated and breathless, and flung an arm around Billy's shoulders, trying to keep it friendly looking while giving it a little private squeeze. "That was awesome! A thousand-year-old dance. Just imagine how much better it could be with everyone in early medieval kit and an authentic band. You can bet our rival society doesn't have anything like this. And there's nothing like a desire to one-up that lot to motivate the lads."

Billy smiled, perhaps at his enthusiasm or perhaps at the touch on his shoulder. "I've been thinking too." His voice and face were raised, as though he meant to say this to the whole side. Martin had a sudden flash of fear that maybe the near-hug had given him the idea that it was okay for the Griffins to know, and he was going to announce their private business to everyone.

He dropped the shoulder clasp at once and linked his hands around his beer mug. Evening midges were out now, tickling along his cheeks and down his back. Alternatively, the crawling sensation might be fear.

"Matt, I wanted to . . ." Billy began.

But Matt was talking to Graham, and Annette was talking to the Boy. Colin had disappeared again to watch the football on the pub's big-screen TV, and no one was listening to Billy. Not listening to him *again*. Still not listening.

It might be shooting himself in the foot, but Martin didn't currently care. He hated to see Billy treated like he didn't exist. "Matt?" he said, touching the guy's elbow to get his attention. "Billy had something to say."

Billy pinked up across the nose at that, his smile practically glowing, and Martin felt so proud he was almost prepared to be outed then and there.

"You remember when we were dancing at the Spread Eagle in Stretham?"

Matt sat down with a flicker of gaze towards Martin that he couldn't quite parse. Annette and the Boy turned in their places to listen.

"There were lots of sides in black face, and that black lady had to drive through the middle of all of us in her car?"

"I remember." Annette looked at Martin too, uncomfortable, a little guilty. "She looked so threatened, poor woman. She must have thought we were mocking her."

Martin caught his breath. Well, well, it took a while but things percolated under the surface, sometimes.

"I know we say, 'It's authentic,'" Billy went on, his voice apologetic but firm. "But we've already mucked around with the kit—you wouldn't see any nineteenth-century plough boys wearing top hats and raven feathers and steampunk goggles. So why not muck around with the face paint too?"

He turned to Martin almost fiercely, in a strange, exalted mood, as if he didn't know whether he was thrilled or terrified. "Would it still be an insult if our faces had red and black patterns? Like the red arrow we have down our spines? Because then it would still be a disguise, but it just wouldn't be offensive."

Martin was struck speechless. He had been expecting the dismissal of his desires and fears, coercion to see things their way, to stop making trouble. That was how his own family expressed love after all—forcing him into things he didn't want. This was *so much better*.

As he dropped his face into his hands to try to conceal how moved he was, Annette covered for him with what seemed deliberate grace. "I could have red roses on top of the black. I could have a face full of red roses. How marvellously strange!"

"Boy?" Matt asked.

Billy leaned in to whisper, "Are you okay?" in Martin's ear. "I thought you'd be happy. Did I get it wrong?"

"The whole thing's made up in my opinion," the Boy grumbled. "Red, black, half and half, I don't care."

"I'm so . . ." Martin murmured, trying to find a way to say how touched he was. But he couldn't manage it here where he was being observed. "Can we go home now? I want to kiss you."

"Graham?"

"Rather fancy being Rorschach, actually. So yes, I'm for it."

"Well then, we'll make that a new rule," said Matt with a brisk air. "If that's better, Martin?"

"It really is." Martin stood up and offered his hand for a handshake, not knowing a less sentimental way of saying *You've justified my faith in human nature*. "Thank you."

"And thank you," he said later, as he and Billy turned into the shade of the churchyard yews on the way back to Billy's house, and he pulled Billy into a long, melting kiss. "You have no idea what a weight that is off my mind. You're the best man alive, Billy Wright. I hope you know that. I'm going to try to say it often enough that you never forget."

CHAPTER SIXTEEN

The twentieth of June, a Friday, and Billy woke with the knowledge that it was going to be a good day. When he drew back his blackout curtains, it was to deep-blue sky with a few fluffy clouds. The wheat was ripening, and the golden flowers of the oilseed rape fields were beginning to fall, green fields becoming yellow, yellow fields turning green in a slow, fresh seesaw of colour. The roses were out in the hedgerows, and under one of the churchyard yews a small red fox sat, licking its paw and glancing up to meet his eye when he slid the window open to let in cool sunshine.

He was light today. The muscles of his legs were springy, the inside of his chest was free of lead. He thought he knew what Martin meant about the joys of taking chain mail off. Depression was a heavy thing, but on the days when it wasn't weighing him down, he felt like he could fly.

Martin didn't cure the depression. Billy still had good days and bad, and during the week, when Martin wasn't there, it was sometimes all he could do to put on clothes, make it to the sofa with a box of cereal and a cup of tea, snag his laptop, and browse eBay all day long while waiting for Martin to Skype. But there was something about the man that made even those days easier. Even the worst of his doubts could not convince him that Martin was only pretending to care about him.

He'll realize soon that you're impossible to love, was all they could manage, though that was bad enough. *Just think how much more it's going to hurt when he leaves. How are you going to manage then?*

Speaking of Martin... Billy snapped himself out of that potential downward spiral, made himself coffee, and found his phone, leaning a bare hip against the kitchen counter as he speed-dialled Martin's number. It gave him a tiny frisson of joy to listen to Martin's sleepy "Martin Deng?" while walking around his flat altogether in the nude.

"Hi," he said, "it's me." That was ... yeah. For a moment there he'd overlooked the fact that people forgot him when he wasn't present. Automatically, his lips shaped his own name as he prepared to remind Martin of his existence.

"Billy." Martin's sleepy slur warmed and sharpened, and Billy hugged himself with one arm in happiness at the thought that Martin recognised his voice and was glad to hear it. "You okay?"

"I'm fine." Billy frowned, not sure if he was imagining things or if Martin really did sound down. "How are you?"

"Oh, I'm all right, I suppose."

No, that was definitely down: surly, self-pitying, borderline aggressive.

He doesn't want to hear from you. I told you so.

"What's the matter?"

Martin's sigh sounded like a distant sea. There was a noise of shuffling—he must be pushing the bedclothes back, maybe getting up. They were both standing alone, naked, disgruntled, and Billy had never felt more acutely the wish that he could be giving someone a hug.

"Three rejections yesterday, and today my severance pay runs out." Martin's voice had grown flatter, some of its smooth depths replaced with hollowness. "I could fucking scream, to be honest. Scream and shout and hit something, except I know it wouldn't help."

Because it was a good day, Billy understood that it wasn't about him at all, that Martin was not upset with him. He sighed in relief and then felt guilty about being happy about the way in which Martin was down.

He didn't think twice before saying, "Listen, I know it's Friday, but how would it be if you came over? Straight away. We could go into town. There's a bookshop in Trowchester that might have something about ancient music. I played fiddle at a wedding yesterday, so I have a bit of cash. I could treat you to lunch out."

Martin sighed again, like a storm wind through a wood. "I should really go and sign on."

"You can do that on Monday," Billy insisted, seized by the thought of walking around the city hand in hand with Martin, people looking and envying him, people looking and knowing they belonged together. "I think you ought to know I'm standing here without a stitch of clothes on, thinking about you."

The flatness in Martin's tone eased. "Yeah?"

"Yes. Wouldn't it be better if we were naked together instead of apart?"

Martin laughed. "You've got me there. I'll be around in about an hour and a half, packed for the weekend."

"I'll be waiting."

Kaminski wouldn't answer the door, Mrs. Webb couldn't, so Billy judged it safe to pad downstairs later when he heard the sound of an approaching engine and open the door in the nude.

When he came inside, Martin's expression took a sudden, comical turn from wearily grim to incredulous. His gaze swept Billy from the top of his head to his feet and back up again more lazily as he licked his parted lips. "You *are* having a good day."

"Mmm." Billy chuckled, taking hold of Martin's arm and tugging him up the stairs. "But still, we'd better not push it." He opened his door with one hand and shoved Martin in with the other, kicking the door closed while Martin stood bewildered on the living room floor.

Martin looked at him as though he didn't know what he was seeing, as Billy hooked his fingers under the other man's T-shirt and pulled it over his head, but the confusion had eased by the time the garment hit the floor. As Billy tackled his belt buckle, Martin stepped in closer so he could rub a hand across Billy's chest, flicking a nipple with a sting and surge of delight.

"This is you as I first met you," Martin said, wonderingly. "That cocky, springy bastard that danced a 'fuck you' to my whole army. Don't get me wrong, I love you when you're quiet, and when you need me, but God, I missed this."

Billy undid Martin's trousers, sunk to his knees, pulling them down with him. As he bent his head to unlace Martin's shoes, Martin laid a hand on his shoulder to support himself and lifted first one foot then the other so Billy could free him of trousers and boxers, shoes and socks.

I love you, Billy thought, swallowing around a sudden lump in his throat, wondering if it had been a slip of the tongue. If it had been meant. If it was only for this Billy and not the other. He rested his cheek against Martin's thigh a moment, then slid his hands up to get a grip on Martin's hips, relishing the solid, sturdy strength of them, kissed up Martin's inner thigh until he could lick the crease between groin and leg, lave Martin's balls with long smooth strokes of his tongue.

Martin growled low in his chest, and Billy smiled as he was taken by the hair, his face tilted up so he could lick along the shaft of Martin's prick. He looked up as he sucked it into his mouth, saw Martin gazing down, dazed and flushed and happy. *I did that*, he thought. *Maybe I can't fight my own sadness, but his doesn't stand a chance against me.*

It was a good feeling. Powerful. He smiled as far as he could without baring his teeth and plunged in, filling his mouth and throat with Martin's heat, choking himself on cock as he swallowed to get it further down.

Martin cried out, his hips jerking forward, his knees almost giving way. When he caught himself, straightened up, his fingers wound into fists in Billy's hair, tightening almost painfully. Billy laughed for joy, and Martin cried out again at the vibration around his shaft, holding Billy still and fucking his mouth, gently at first and then wilder as Billy gave him little moaning grunts of encouragement, digging his fingers into Martin's arse and clinging on tighter.

When Martin came, Billy managed to swallow most of it, just a little trickle escaping from the corner of his mouth, sliding down to pool in the hollow of his collarbone.

"Oh. Oh," Martin panted, catching his breath, and then he swiped his fingers through the goo, and collapsing down, curling around Billy, he brought him off with long firm strokes of his wet hand, their cum mingling on his fingers as Billy came hard almost instantly at the touch.

Billy snuggled into Martin's body as it surrounded him, raised his arms to lock around Martin's waist, tucked his face into Martin's shoulder, and gave himself up to a long moment of satiated bliss, warm and sticky and safe. Smug too, because for once in his life he was pretty sure he'd done well.

They lay a long time, curled together, blissed out, while Billy enjoyed the sensation of Martin's breathing as it lifted his chest and belly, rocking Billy to and fro with each inhale and exhale. He must have closed his eyes and drowsed a little, because Martin was shaking him lightly when he opened them again. The carpet was suddenly rough and prickly under his knees, and his spilled cum had turned tacky.

"Hey." Martin shook him again. "Shower time, before we're glued together."

Billy smiled up at him, stretching, feeling as energized as if he'd had a good night's sleep. "Okay. You scrub my back, and I'll do yours?"

"And the front too. Call it a special offer." Martin got stiffly to his feet, helping pull Billy up with him. His eyes had brightened since he walked through the door and the lines of tension on his face had eased.

Billy could imagine it as the face of a pharaoh—the same tip-tilted almond eyes and the strong but elegant lines he'd seen before in the statue of Khafre, on whom the Sphinx was modelled. It gave him a chill to think that maybe, maybe through Martin's father there really was a link there, back into twenty thousand years of civilized power.

He laughed. "It's a deal. Then breakfast and then we go out."

An hour later, still sleek and glowing from the shower, they stepped off the Rosebery Wood bus into the walled market town of Trowchester.

"Who on earth are all of these?" Martin asked, as the fourth dreadlocked, woad-painted aspiring Celt pushed past them, beating a dull rhythm on a heavily painted bodhran.

Billy looked out from the bus stop with a sinking feeling. The place was heaving. A small tribe of Picts, no doubt lost fifteen centuries ago in the depths of an enchanted forest, had reemerged and were sitting on the pavements all around the Salmon of Wisdom fish-and-chip shop. They were clad in colourful rags of clothing probably woven in Nepal. Uniformly, their hair was long and matted and sometimes multicoloured, their skin the hard worn brown of people who do not have regular access to baths.

A man with a beard like Merlin and the caste mark of a Brahmin was lazily playing the didgeridoo, while the bodhran player gamely attempted to accompany him, but couldn't quite work out the rhythm.

Billy's carefully honed musicianship winced as he tried to filter it out.

"Oh. It's coming up to the summer solstice. I forgot."

"Forgot?" Martin took his elbow, which gave him such a hit of pride and pleasure that he almost didn't mind when across the street a Scottish piper in full regalia struck up "Molly Malone" on the bagpipes. The piper was perhaps attempting to drown out the didgeridoo, but all that happened was that his rhythm formed a third in the disharmonious, out-of-time racket.

Billy flinched and headed up the street away from them all as fast as humanly possible, Martin trailing after, looking concerned. "Yeah. We have a Bronze Age hill fort, locally known as Wednesday Keep." He gestured at the skyline just to the right of the castle on its conical hill, and Martin dropped his elbow as he turned to look.

"A hill fort?"

"Don't you know this stuff? We're only an hour's drive away from where you live. It's practically your back doorstep."

Rather than take his arm again when they began walking, Martin pushed his hands into his jeans pockets, alternating looking where he was going with little glances up at the mysterious past he couldn't quite see from here.

The sound of the pipes faded as Billy strode up the old paved high street, but the crowds didn't thin. A motorcycle gang were revving their engines outside Marks and Spencer, laughing pointedly at the backs of a snake of dancing Hare Krishna devotees, all with hand drums and bells around their ankles.

The noise itched up his back and got itself under his hair, began working down through the layers of his skin. The orbit of his right eye grew tight with the tension that preceded a headache. He dropped closer to Martin, needing his solid, sturdy presence as the world shivered with too much input around him. Martin helped make things quiet.

"History has always been my thing..." Martin looked up at him with a rueful smile. "But I've mostly ignored geography. Has there been a dig there? Is there a museum?"

"Both." A car went by with its windows open and the relentless beat of dubstep pulsing out, shaking the air around Billy, shaking the particles that made up his body. Out of time. Out of time with everything else. He was beginning to feel sick.

He bowed forward and pressed his hands over his ears, but all that did was bring to mind how bright everything was. Planters hung off the lampposts up the street, garish with flowers. All the windows glittered. The clothes outside the hippy shops were covered in flames where stitched-on mirrors reflected the glaring sky. The colours of the cobbles were supersaturated, and he could see every particle of dirt like a boulder, jagged-edged and in his way.

"Billy?" Martin took his arm again, which helped. He tried sliding his hand up, but he had barely got his fingers intertwined with Martin's before Martin was pulling away, looking around himself as if afraid he'd been spotted doing something dire.

Right, Billy thought, remembering with a shock of desolation, *he's ashamed of me. He's ashamed to have anyone see that he's with me. And who can blame him?*

He did, though. He shut his eyes and firmed his mouth and waited in his own private darkness for disappointment and overload to ease up alike.

"Billy, are you okay?"

Fat lot you care, Billy thought, as Martin's arm came around his waist. Not like a lover—that would have been welcome—but like a man supporting his mate when he's too drunk or high to walk on his own.

They shambled forward, through an oppressive noise-scape in which the shrill tones of an ice-cream van jarred against Radio 2's Golden Hour and canned wolf song and panpipes and fifty different conversations at once and footsteps and snapping flags overhead and two jets high in the summer sky and pub jukebox music and car engines and a horn and the bagpiper still droning, and someone saying something about bookshops and how could they expect him to filter it all out and make sense of it when it was under his fucking skin and under his skull and inside his bones and he couldn't, he couldn't . . .

He drove a foot hard into some kind of step. "Come on, up here," Martin said quietly, his voice still blessedly rounded and right. Billy raised his foot, passed over some kind of threshold. The light shining in his face dimmed and some of the tense, aching panic passed out of his muscles. Then there was a definite, pointed snick, and the cacophony stopped.

Taking his hands away from his ears, he found he could still hear it, reduced to a distant, manageable murmur. He covered his eyes instead and sucked in the scent of dehumidified air and coconut matting, coffee and paper and books.

Martin guided him across a second threshold and then pushed him down onto a padded bench, where he bent forward, pulled his knees up, and hugged himself tight, taking long, deep breaths of relief.

"I'm sorry," Martin murmured to someone. It sounded like he was standing between the newcomer and Billy, guardian-like and protective. "It was just a little ... hectic, I think."

"Oh, Lord, it's a zoo out there," came a man's voice in reply. The faint Irish accent, lilting and amused, soothed down some of Billy's raised prickles. He began to uncurl. "I don't blame you at all. You'll be wanting something to drink, I expect. Let me see what I have."

"That's very kind of you," said Martin, and the stranger laughed.

"No, no. It's not kindness, I assure you. I'm just guilting you into buying a book before you leave. I make no bones about that."

Billy took another breath of the soft air and opened his eyes in time to catch the disappearance of a small, dapper-looking man as he ducked through to the hallway and the flight of steps there. Then Martin lowered himself onto the window seat where Billy had been deposited. Looking round first to make sure they were alone, he took Billy's hands in his.

It would have been a more touching gesture if it hadn't been so furtive, but something inside Billy unfurled at it regardless.

"Are you all right?"

Billy nodded, feeling more solid by the second, the bookshop's cool silence soothing his aching head and shredded nerves. He tried his voice, and it held firm. "Yes. It was a bit much but ... Sorry. I was telling you about the hill fort. There's a dig going on up there now—"

"I would love to take part in one of those." Martin shuffled closer, so that Billy could put his head down on his shoulder. "It must be so exciting, turning up things that no one has touched but you for thousands of years."

"Mmm." Even Martin was not immune to interrupting him, apparently, but he was still too grateful for the reprieve to object. "There's also a spring up there, which some crackpot in Victorian times claimed was where the waters of Urd's well push up from the underworld."

As expected, Martin gave him a sceptical grimace, his look of frozen worry beginning to melt back into enjoyment. "I'm pretty sure there's no mention of that in the sagas."

Billy gave a little huff of amusement, pleased to find it didn't aggravate his head. The ache was fading. He was going to be fine. "Maybe not, but various movements got hold of the idea in the sixties, so now it's a place of pilgrimage. We're not quite Glastonbury yet, but we're getting there."

Martin laughed too, tilting his head so that his cheek rested against Billy's hair. "So that's why your little town's full of 'alternative' types? I rather like it, to be honest. It's interesting."

"They're book lovers, most of them. The more obscure the better. Free thinkers. You have to admire that in a man."

Billy jumped and then scowled as Martin let go of his hands and scrambled away to put a modest foot of distance between them. The stranger, having reappeared in a silence appropriate for an assassin, raised his eyebrows and gave Billy a sympathetic look. "I'm sorry to startle you. Here, drinks."

They smelled of hedgerows. Elderflower cordial, with bubbles fizzing over the surface of the pale-yellow liquid. They tasted sweet and green, as cooling as the bookshop's shade.

"Better?" The little man's mossy green eyes watched them both with amusement. Faded freckles dusted the bridge of his aquiline nose and were echoed on his spotted waistcoat. "Then can I interest you in a book? I run the best—though sadly the only—gay book club in Trowchester if you happen to have nothing to do on a Friday evening."

Billy caught the man's eye and couldn't help smiling at the obvious support, the well-executed needling. Ignoring Martin's obvious discomfort, he held out his hand to be shaken. "Billy Wright. I live in Rosebery Wood, but I might just do that if I can make the buses work."

"Fintan Hulme." The man gathered up the bookshop with a gesture. "This is my kingdom, in which lovers are always welcome."

Ooh, rub it in, Billy thought as he watched Martin's face grow rigid, and then crumple into hot embarrassment. "Thank you," he said. "It's nice. It's so nice, when people aren't ashamed of you."

He felt a certain amount of unworthy glee when Martin frowned at that, because he didn't want to be invisible, relegated to the shadows like a dirty secret. But then he also felt guilty because the purpose of today was not to make Martin feel worse.

"Do you have anything on ancient music? Specifically Saxon and Viking tunes . . ." He paused to think, "Or ancient Egyptian and African ones. Ideally I'm looking for sheet music, but anything that can be adapted to be played would do."

Fintan went still, the humour disappearing from his eyes in favour of something calculating, cataloguing. Billy had the impression he was flicking through some internal card index.

"I'm not ashamed of you," Martin leaned in close to whisper in Billy's ear. "I explained—"

"You explained why Ametel can't do it while he's being a scary Viking, though frankly if it bothers you, I don't mind pretending to be your war captive or whatever." Billy's own temper was getting in the way of his good day now. "You never explained why Martin can't. But . . . but never mind. I don't want to waste an up day on being angry. I understand why I'm not much of a catch. Why you don't want to be seen with me."

"That's not it either!" Martin exclaimed, only to be interrupted by a mocking tut from Fintan Hulme.

"I have the very volume you're looking for, lads, if you're still together enough at the end of this conversation to want it."

The thought that they might be straying into breakup territory sobered Billy immediately. "I think we're done with this conversation for today."

Martin smiled, looking reprieved and grateful and a little shiny-eyed, as though Billy was his hero. "Thank you."

But when they were leaving and Martin had ducked through the door, its spring closing it slowly behind him, Fintan touched Billy's elbow and stopped him long enough to say, "Don't let him walk all over what you want. If it's important to you, stand up for it. He'll thank you, in the end."

"I . . ." Billy wasn't sure about this complete stranger giving him advice. It felt bracing for a moment, as though everything really was that simple, and maybe it was for this little man. Maybe he was the kind of person who could insist on having things his own way and fight until it happened.

But you're not, are you? You're too weak for that.

"I have so many other things I need my strength for at the moment," he said, sounding about as pathetic as he felt. "This can wait."

Fintan looked at him sharply, as if he had heard Billy's inner voice for himself. Then he shrugged and smiled. "Of course you shouldn't tackle it until you're ready. But do come on Friday. We're very good with tea and prying, and we run a fine stable of contract killers if you find you should need one."

Billy laughed, surprised, and pushed the door open again with a feeling that something had shifted in his chest. Apparently it wasn't just him who thought it was unacceptable to have to live your life pretending not to love the person you loved. It *was* unacceptable, and he therefore was allowed not to accept it.

He had no idea what to do with this revelation because after all he didn't want to tell Martin it was the closet or him, but it made him feel oddly solid inside as he set foot back into the overstimulating day, and that was really rather nice.

CHAPTER
SEVENTEEN

"This is not as scratchy as I feared." Annette plucked at the sleeves of her Saxon gown, trying to pull them down to cover her wrists. As they were cut short to reveal the skintight linen sleeves of the under-dress, this was a fruitless endeavour.

"You look great in it." Billy struggled with leg bindings—straps of brightly woven wool that he was supposed to wind around his calves to hold his trouser bottoms tight against his leg and protect them from briars and wear. "It's very dignified, and surprisingly flattering."

The Saxon dress was mostly but not quite like the dress from *Brave*. Tight on the torso, with loose sleeves that came down to the elbow, from which the contrasting tight sleeves of the under-dress protruded in a flash of colour. From the hips, the dress's skirt flared out in a bell wide enough for Annette to stride, had she wished to. Its hem ended at the midcalf, so that the fuller skirt of the under-dress could be seen in pleasing ruffles beneath it. Even that ended just above the ground, so Annette could walk without fear of tripping.

On her head she wore a headdress that Billy associated more with nuns—a white cap to cover all her hair, and a loose white hood, pinned to the cap, which covered her neck and shoulders.

"Well, I feel ridiculous," she said, fussing again with the cuffs. "I'm far too old to be dressing up like Maid Marian."

"You look more like Queen Emma." Martin ducked into the tent where they were wrestling with their borrowed costumes. Outside, the dim light of an English summer diffused through heavy cloud. It was raw and wet-cold, a thin drizzle blowing picturesquely over the grounds of Dover Castle.

Martin, as always, wore his Viking clothes as casually as if he had grown up in them. He had developed little, unconscious movements to control them—a shrug to keep the cloak folded properly over one shoulder, a brushing motion to manage the skirts without getting his knees tangled in them.

"There's a manuscript illustration of her presenting a golden cross to Hyde Abbey, and you're the spitting image of it. Are we nearly ready? The English Heritage rep just told me they want it indoors in quarter of an hour. The ground's too slippery for the jousting, so we've got their timeslot. The organisers have opened up the great hall to fit us and the public in together."

Billy forced down an instinctive trill of nerves and terror. "Wow. So we've got to make it up to all the people who only came for the jousting?"

"Absolutely. And all the people who only came to walk round the gardens in the sun."

"They'll be glad of us." Annette gave up on trying to push the headdress out of her peripheral vision and picked up the kantele she was borrowing. It nestled like a baby kangaroo in a furry pouch designed to protect it. "When you go to a stately home for a day out, all you really need is some entertainment and a cream tea afterwards. We'll be saving all those paying guests a day of disappointment. We couldn't have a better chance."

"No pressure, then." Billy forced down his apprehension with a joke. But Martin seemed to notice the anxiety nevertheless. Martin made a habit of noticing things. It was what Billy had first loved about him.

"You okay?"

Billy shook his head and smiled, swallowing down dread. "Our first show. It's a big moment. I just don't want to stuff it up."

"But you won't."

"I know. Anyway, it's not me is it?" Billy waved a hand at himself, now clothed like a ninth-century peasant in cream trousers and yellow tunic. "It's this guy, Ivald. I don't care too much if *he* comes out of this looking like a prat."

Martin laughed. "Yeah. We both know something about the power of masks, right? I get what you mean. I'm going to go rustle up the others. See you in the great hall in ten minutes."

Billy watched Martin duck through the tent flap and hurry away. There was a roll in his gait as though he was a sailor newly put ashore, and he moved a little stiffly, but he'd still proved to be an enthusiastic and accurate dancer. He was quick to learn the steps, making up in strength and vigour what he lacked in grace. Billy quite liked it—Martin danced like a man, and morris suited that.

"So." Annette ducked her head and gave Billy a knowing look from under her lashes. "Things are going well between you two?"

The stage fright disappeared beneath a wash of embarrassed pleasure. Billy picked up his own sheepskin bag full of instrument and fiddled with the toggles that closed it, but he couldn't quite help the big ridiculous smile. "I didn't think anyone had twigged that we were together."

"Oh, come on. Even if you didn't keep gazing at him as though he was the only man on earth, we seem to have had a season where every show we attended, Bretwalda were there too. Since you and he are the ones who arrange the calendars, that's a giveaway even without this joint venture."

"I suppose."

"When are you going to get him to come and dance with the Griffins? We could always do with more dancers."

Billy still felt the solidity beneath the breastbone that he had gained in Trowchester bookshop—the feeling that there was a line over which he would not step. But God, he had bent it as far as it was humanly possible to do so, and it hadn't done any good anyway. Annette still knew.

"I should probably tell you that Martin's kind of in the closet about being gay. He doesn't want anyone to know. Are you saying the whole side's aware of it already?"

That was a step in the right direction, if so. If Martin could be out when he was around Billy, then Billy wouldn't mind so much if he was in everywhere else.

"I assume so." Annette tugged again at her sleeves, looking concerned. "I thought it was common knowledge. I may have . . . well, passed the assumption on. Is that going to cause you problems?"

Rather than look at her friendly, guilty face, Billy stepped out of the tent and led the way over water-grey grass, past canvas shelters in which you could just make out the shadows of Vikings authentically huddling round the fire. A few hardy members of the public, looking forlorn under their umbrellas, walked disconsolately through the ghost town, or stood by the lists reading the notice announcing that the jousting had been cancelled. Martin's Kayleigh, her kit now looking more seasoned, her stance easier and her expressions more confident, was going from one group to the next, directing them up to the castle.

"I…" Billy's nerves began vibrating like plucked strings with hope and incredulity. "Not as far as I'm concerned. But maybe we'd better stop the side from telling anyone in Bretwalda." No, actually this was good. Martin could practice being out while he was at Billy's, and once he'd realized for himself how much better it was, it might just spread, automatically, into other areas of his life.

Because he'd been having interesting, daring thoughts about the money pit that was Martin's flat, all those days spent away from Billy that were making Martin look fretful and thin. All those days Martin spent away, that brought home to Billy how echoingly empty his own flat was without the man, how much he was beginning to resent all the moments he spent apart from him.

Billy wasn't sure if saying this aloud would jinx it, but he wanted to tell someone, so that the idea would be out there in the world for real. "I've been thinking about asking him to move in. He's got money troubles, no job. It makes sense for him to sell his flat, come and live with me. If I can nerve myself up to ask him, then yes, you can bet I'll bring him to practice too. It'll be great that he can be himself with the side. But in the mean time we'd better tell them to keep it quiet, all right?"

The castle's entrance hall was no warmer than outside, but it was at least considerably drier. Billy walked down a corridor lined by threadbare carpet, absorbing with shamefaced pleasure the glances and interest of the other people also on the way to the great hall.

Through a carved oak doorway, he came out into a space as airy and gracefully proportioned as a timber-framed barn. A huge fireplace of white stone blackened by immemorial soot opened along one side of the room. Only five feet of the hearth was taken up by a fire, but this had clearly been burning all day, the ember-bed deep and bright, apple-wood logs on top of it leaping with sweet-scented flames.

High mullioned windows let in the rain-dim light, and showed faded blue-and-crimson murals painted on the walls, bright gold-leaf stars aglitter above among the rafters. Shreds of banners stirred in the rising heat, and every person who'd come to the estate for a pleasant day out, only to be thwarted by the rain, was crammed around the edges of a hastily roped-off area in the middle of the chequerboard floor.

The rest of the Early Dance Group were clustered together as far from the fire as they could get. Billy's stage fright calmed at the sight of Martin. There was something about Martin that seemed to trail calm with it, that eased his constant anxiety and told him he would be all right. He wasn't sure it was telling the truth, but it was a lie he was rapidly beginning to depend on.

Billy and the other musicians, Christine, Annette, and Martin's Stigand on the bone spoons, filed into the arena, bowed to the crowds and then sat down on one edge, so that they would not block anyone's view.

Annette drew a shivery, silver tune from the kantele that silenced the talking all around them. Even with synthesizers, there was nothing in modern life that sounded like the kantele. Its sharp, pure notes floated from metal strings that, once plucked, continued to reverberate through the wood of the instrument, through the air, without ending. The tune seemed to float above an unbearably sweet, bell-like voice that sang in counterpoint.

It was eerie as hell.

Rain tapped on the glass of the windows, and inside the hall, the crowd were holding their breath. The fire sighed and settled and the voice of a metal angel filled all the great spaces with beauty and awe.

It didn't seem that the final note ever ended, only that it passed into realms the human ear could not hear, and continued there, holy and untouchable.

Martin walked out into the silence. "Welcome lords and ladies, churls and thralls. If you were here before the downpour, you may have seen the combat display put on by my society, Bretwalda. And if you wait until four this afternoon, you'll see the Stomping Griffins morris side, dancing in a tradition that came to this country in the fifteenth century. When I first saw them, it made me realize that we put a lot of effort into thinking about warfare in earlier times, and nowhere near enough into reenacting the things that made life worth living. The things that the warriors gave their lives to defend. I wanted to see if we could recreate the lost dances of the Vikings in the same way we re-create their battles.

"What you see today are the fruits of that attempt. I hope you'll go easy on us. This is our first event. First of all, I want to tell you about the instruments. Before I describe each one, our musician will give you a short solo. Then I'll tell you about the research that went into the creation of the dances and we will demonstrate those. Then questions. And then, if there's still time after that, we'll get you involved with a simple circle dance to stir your blood and take away the cold.

"So, that amazing sound you just heard was a kantele..."

Martin had a slow, confident, authoritative delivery. Billy could see why he had gone into teaching—he combined a genuine enthusiasm for his subject with a gift for making it understandable. And he had a practised eye in reading when a crowd had all the information they could take in one go and needed to be loosened up with some entertainment.

It went superbly. The crowd pushed in close enough to the dancers to feel the ground shake beneath their feet, to feel the visceral tug of movement and effort and skill as they would never have done had they been watching it at a distance. A roar of laughter and applause greeted the finale when they filled the hall with four circles of dancers, one inside the other, rotating in opposite directions. Just for a moment, it clicked, and everyone felt the synergy, the perfection. When it fell apart, the onlookers left with glowing faces, chattering excitedly to one another, rain forgotten.

A besuited woman seized Billy's arm as he was putting the hearpe to bed in its woolly coat. Even the unwanted touch couldn't put a dent in his satisfaction. "You're the cofounder of this group?"

"That's right."

"I'm Nicky Riley." She pushed her ultra-fashionable glasses firmly into the bridge of her nose. "The events manager for English Heritage."

This time she offered a handshake where he could spot the touch coming. One of those annoying, halfhearted shakes, where her hand curled into his, making it impossible to establish a firm grip. "Hi."

"I loved your solo, by the way. Were the lyrics from *Beowulf*?"

"From 'The Wanderer,'" Billy corrected her gently, offering a translation, "'Where are the horse and the rider? Where is the giver of gifts? Where now are the seats at the feast and the revels in the hall? Alas for the bright cup! Alas for the warrior in his byrnie! Alas for the sovereign's splendour! Now that time has passed away—dark under night-shadow—as if it had never been.'"

Billy ducked his head in embarrassment. "I thought it would please the Tolkien fans, as well as being fitting somehow for this place. It looks like it's seen a few revels in its time that it doesn't see anymore."

"Yes, well, we're working on that," she said, smiling a thin smile. She had a size zero waiflike quality to her, but her voice was all Oxbridge confidence as she passed him a clipboard containing a long list of other events. "And we're always looking for things that can be done indoors. Could your group be available for any of these events? And if so, where can we go to talk about money?"

CHAPTER EIGHTEEN

"After the disaster in town at midsummer, I thought this would be better." Billy shrugged the rucksack with their picnic in it further up his back and tightened the straps. He had paused just before the first stile that punctuated the hardest path up Wednesday Hill, waiting for Martin to disengage himself from a passing family's friendly red setter and follow him over.

Martin raised his head to look at him. His eyes were clearer than they had been when he arrived, and his body had opened up like a hedgehog uncurling when the threat has passed. "I really shouldn't take money from the Early Dance Group to pay for my petrol. I feel kind of shit about that. But on the other hand I was going mad at home. Three more rejections and a 'come for a further interview in a month.' A month!"

Billy had a lifestyle in which he need never hold down a steady job. The money would keep coming in even if he lay in bed for a fortnight. He considered himself very fortunate, especially when watching what the extended period of joblessness and stress was doing to Martin.

The guy had been the picture of confidence when they'd met. Now he spoke more softly. His back was bowed. He occupied less space when he sat, and it took a special effort like this from Billy to remove the creases of his permanent frown from his forehead.

"Well, I thought I'd show you the sacred well, and some of the hill fort. James may even be there."

The dog leapt up and licked Martin's face in good-bye, then bounded off to follow its people. Martin straightened with a smile. "James?"

"He's a member of that book club Finn told us about." Billy clambered over the boot-polished step of the stile and landed on dusty wood chippings on the other side. When he was a boy, the path had been nothing but a scraping in the earth, a palm's width of rubbed-off grass in the summer, a muddy drain in the winter. Trowchester council had obviously decided its tourists needed better than that.

"The gay book club?" Martin made heavy weather of getting over the fence, obviously unpractised in the art of navigating the countryside. His frown had returned, and it twinged something resentful and angry in Billy's chest.

"Yes," he said. "The gay book club. I thought I would go because I am gay. You are too, in case you hadn't noticed."

Martin gaped at him for a moment, perhaps taken aback by the unfamiliar note of anger in Billy's tone. Then he lunged forward and wrapped both arms tight round Billy's chest. He pushed his face into Billy's neck and held on. The embrace was too tight, making Billy's chest hurt, making him feel sorry that he ever raised the subject, sorry for being difficult and demanding at a time when Martin was already going through enough.

"I'm sorry," Martin said into his collarbone. "I didn't mean that to come out how it sounded. Not accusing. It's just . . . you know. I know you want me to be open about this. I know you want me to be out. And I'm going to be. That is the plan. Long-term. But I don't want to jinx my chances of getting a job. All it takes is one bigoted parent raising an unfounded scare about homosexuals and paedophilia and a school could find itself in more shit than it wants to handle, so of course they're going to go for the uncontroversial option and find someone straight—white too. My dad is disappointed enough with me already. I just . . . I can't face it, Billy, not right now."

Martin smelled of citrus from his shower gel, and his arms were warm and strong. Billy let himself relax into them and relish the way they drove away his own demons. God, he hoped Martin's current down was not his fault. Hoped that he was not somehow feeding off the man's strength, sapping his will to do the things that scared him. Could that happen?

Billy sighed, and as he breathed in again, his lungs were filled with the scent of trees, with that leaf-mulch and high-oxygen thrill of the woods. Maybe this argument could wait. Billy could wait a little longer, couldn't he, before he decided Martin's closet was an unbearable place to be? He felt strong today, but he wasn't sure he felt strong enough to have that fight Finn recommended.

"All right," he said and kissed Martin's eyebrow and the tip of his nose, making him smile. "Come on."

You're going to give in forever, you know. You always do. You have no fucking backbone at all. He's never going to change, you're never going to change. You're going to carry on being dishonest for the rest of your life.

But the peace and the trees held him up, and it was another good day, and he could let that part of him ramble on to itself, a little grimy, a little wearying, but ignorable for now.

They trekked uphill again, through groves of hazel where the nuts were beginning to form. On into the deeper forest trees, bent oak and brave ashes and sycamore heavy with seeds like helicopters. Sun filtered down in shafts of heavenly gold, and as they went their strides opened out, and a blush of exertion came to Martin's cheeks.

The path took a quick dog-leg around a jutting outcrop of rock, and then the hillside came closer on the left, the ground tilting up into a sheer face of grey stone in which ferns and the roots of bent little hardy trees were anchored like grappling irons. The land to their right began to slope down, glimpses of retreating views and sky showing through gaps in the branches. They heard the sound of water, intermittent and untrustworthy, over the sound of the trees.

And then the path swung hard left and the rock wall opened out into a grotto, an almost circular space in the cliff, as though nature had meant to create a tower room and forgotten to give it a roof. The ground had turned to wet red clay, sticky with the prints of thousands of hiking boots.

In the inner curve of the wall, a hole gaped, about the size of a football. From its upper arch, where a long green fern hung, several unimpressive dribbles tinked into the lower, where the water formed a hand-sized pool before spilling over the lip and onto the ever-wet ground.

"Is that a severed head?" Martin asked, squinting up at the faint scratches that surrounded the spring.

Billy was impressed. "Come here." He shoved Martin to the best spot, where the combination of light and shadow would pick out the age-worn carvings most clearly. "Yeah it is. See his long hair and his beard? It's been dated to somewhere in the one thousand BC range. So you can't blame people for thinking it's sacred, even if no one really knows what it means."

Thinking that it was sacred had not stopped people from dropping their rubbish here. Billy picked up crisp packets and Coke cans and empty water bottles as Martin stood in the centre of the stone chimney and soaked up the chill of heavy shade and cold water under the eyes of that drooling face.

They were blessed with a heartbeat of numinous terror and silence before a loudspeaker on the outward track crackled and an enthusiastic voice cried, "And now the sacred well of Urd!" A coachful of tourists in skimpy summer wear and flip-flops emerged from the woods opposite and began sliding unhappily over the blood-red ground.

"This way out." Billy caught Martin's arm and waded through the scrum to the other side of the clearing, where a larger, tarmacked path followed the slope of the hill to where a small car park had been cut in its side.

Billy led Martin through the car park and up the footpath beyond, watching with delight as Martin caught his first glimpse of the hill fort. As they climbed out of the trees, the first wall caught them by surprise, its bank like a moat of shadow under it, its face sheer, still with traces of lime clinging to the stones, making it shine white under its cap of green grass.

"This is fantastic!" Martin exclaimed, all his lines of stress wiped away and a blazing smile in their place. He pushed ahead as the footpath threaded itself through the first bank and ditch, sloped up and curved to pierce the second.

Inside the third circle of battlements on the hill, high above a spectacular view of forest and furze and the red-tiled rooftops of Trowchester set in burgeoning farmland, the tarpaulins and blue plastic that shielded the dig were something of an eyesore. But after walking around the inner bank, surveying the world like the king of this castle, Martin wandered over to them curiously, as Billy had known he would.

A grid of tape had been laid down over a half acre of land in the centre of the fort, measuring sticks at each corner. Two students from the academy were kneeling in opposite corners, one scraping at the dried earth with a trowel, the other brushing fine particles of dirt off something brown.

Although Billy had a lot of respect for archaeology as a discipline, he hadn't really got over his feeling that if it wasn't gold, he didn't want to know. The thing she had found seemed to be a potsherd, which was probably fascinating to those in the know about such things, but it didn't make his heart race. Martin, however, lurched closer as if he'd been pulled, and his expression took on a hint of yearning that made Billy's heart clench.

Be nice if he looked at me like that.

"James not here?" Billy asked the girl with the trowel. He'd hoped that perhaps introducing Martin to a few more openly gay people would help reassure the man that life after coming out was not all that bad.

"A metal detectorist down Hincksley Bottom found something Roman, he said. James had to go off and examine it." She didn't trouble to look up at him, carefully delineating a line of light-brown soil from a line of dark.

"Will he be back today?"

"I don't think so."

Damn.

Martin watched the excavations for another half hour, while Billy found a patch of long grass and cornflowers in which to lie down and bask like a lizard. He would have liked Martin to lie next to him, pliable and warm, so they could sun themselves together and exchange lazy kisses. But when Martin came, he sat a good metre away, obviously conscious of the possibility that the girls might look up and see.

Billy shared out jam sandwiches and crisps, poured the thermos of coffee, and listened to Martin speak about Bronze Age society, with his eyes shining and his limbs loose and his mobile mouth turned up at the ends.

He thought about saying, *Come live with me and be my love*, and the words got trapped somewhere in his lungs, somewhere under his ribs. Because, God, Martin was so beautiful when he was transported like this, with his deep voice rolling like the land, and his mind full of wonderful things that he had to teach, and his hands expressive and strong like the way he danced. He was wonderful, and Billy wanted him to be his.

But he didn't want, he very much didn't want to be invisible in his own life, and Martin threatened to make him that.

So he ate his picnic and sunned himself and said nothing.

In the evening they went home to Billy's and cooked together and ate and laughed over the TV, and planned out the upcoming appearance of Bretwalda, the Griffins, and the Early Dance Group at Hunstanton Country Fair. Still he wanted to tell Martin to stay, so they could keep doing this forever. And still he couldn't make himself say the words.

CHAPTER NINETEEN

Two weeks later and August was confirming that it was a glorious summer. Billy waved the Griffins off in their minibus and stood at the edge of Hunstanton Country Fair, watching the bunting flutter against a stripy red sky as the strong sun finally went down.

In the field in front of him, the lights of a carnival came on, picking out fudge vans and shooting ranges, a merry-go-round of multicoloured horses with curlicued manes, a set of old-fashioned swing boats the colour of crushed topaz, covered with gilding and painted roses.

From the beer tent, the dull rhythmic thud of bass jangled unpleasantly with the nearer steam organ, whose little painted eighteenth-century musician-automatons were dinging tiny bells in time with mechanized Vivaldi. From a nearby stall where you could buy designer wellies, and the yuppie clothes to wear them with, came the sound of Max Bygraves crooning a tune that had probably been popular a half century ago. The combination of all three types of music wound through Billy's bones like an infection, made him feel feverish and nauseous and barely able to breathe.

He blocked his ears and walked closer to the barrier that separated the show ground from the outside world until he was pressed against green-plastic-covered chicken wire and could go no further. Fixing his eyes on the sunset with fierce concentration helped a little. With huge mental effort he *could* block it all out, and it would be worth it. It would be, because he was still kitted up—he had his mask on—and the mask would make him strong enough, reckless enough, to actually ask Martin to move in.

That was the plan, anyway. Martin had had job interviews over the past two weeks that meant he had to return to his flat and stay there. Billy had spent the time wandering around his rooms, deeply aware of how empty they were. The bed was too big to sleep in. Cooking—eating, even—was just not worth the effort if the food couldn't be shared with Martin. He missed the guy from morning to night, and everything was more difficult, everything more of a struggle without him, from summoning the willpower to get out of bed in the morning, to brushing his teeth, to forcing himself out of doors to get to practices. The constant nagging ache of it put his qualms into perspective.

He could deal with being Martin's silent, invisible partner, surely he could. If the alternative was not being Martin's partner at all, then he could deal.

That was his decision. When he had made it, at home, on a morning filled with champagne sunlight washing over night-fresh greenery, in the silence and the emptiness of 6 a.m., it had seemed more achievable than it did now.

Someone shrieked in the beer tent. A jostling knot of young men passed him, swearing and laughing at each other, giving him dirty looks as if there was a law against being overwhelmed by people and noise. He recognised that he was not in the best shape at the moment to execute his plan, that his endurance was coming to an end and a crash was becoming inevitable. He should have gone home, made it to safety before the storm hit.

But you can never get anything right, can you? You've had a lifetime to learn how to manage this and you still can't do it, and that's because you're pathetic.

But he had just waved his transport good-bye. He laced his fingers through the wire, leaned his weight on his arms, and took a deep breath. There seemed very little oxygen in the air; it didn't ease his chest as it should, but he repeated it two, three times, breathing out hard, until he had inflated himself enough to move.

No need to panic. He would go to Martin. Martin was safety. Martin had seen him freak out like this before—no need to fear that this would drive him away. In Martin's tent it would be quieter, or darker, at least, and he could sleep with Martin wrapped around him, keeping it all out. He could put aside the idea of talking about big life choices until the morning, when everything should be easier.

He took another breath, braced himself, and walked back down into the bowl of the field, and the claustrophobic crowd of stalls and strangers.

By the time he got to Bretwalda's encampment, night had fallen properly. The Viking tent village was soothing, a scatter of campfires under canvas awnings, a huddle of cloaked figures around each, lit in subtle shades of umber and gold, talking quietly in lowered voices.

Billy slipped into the back of the work shelter, his bells wrapped in his hankies, silenced in his pockets. He dropped down onto the dry ground, with his back to one of the supports of the table that ran along the side of the shelter. Even though they were facing away from him and had not seen him come in, black-coated and painted-faced in the darkness as he was, the presence of nine other people was an oppression on his spirit like the walls closing in. But the notional solitude of the fact that they didn't know he was here was just enough to keep him breathing.

They took up so much space. There was so little left for him.

You still demand too much. You're still too selfish. You could make yourself smaller if you tried. You just don't care to try because you think you're so wonderful, but you're not.

"I can't believe we're here instead of York," Edith was saying when Billy tuned back in after a long enough period of watching the grass had given him the mental energy to do so. "I mean, it's Jorvik. If they say, 'Come and do an event for us,' we say, 'Right away, how many hundred people do you want?' The chance to work with the Jorvik Viking Centre is—"

"They weren't going to pay us." Martin's voice was deep and soft. Billy would have said there was a silence to it, if he hadn't known that made no sense to anyone but himself. He looked up. Now his eyes were adapted to the dark, he could see that Martin was in a camping chair on the right hand side of the firebox, his feet up on the edge of it, the dew of the evening steaming off his leather shoes. Under such a clear sky even the summer night had an edge to it, and Martin had pulled his woollen cloak tight around him like a cocoon, only his calves in blue-and-yellow leg bindings, and one arm, in which he held a can of beer, protruding from the embroidered material. He looked harassed and guilty.

"I can't afford the petrol to drive all the kit up to York for a show that wasn't even going to pay costs. These people are giving us two hundred pounds."

"We don't do this for the money," Edith protested. "And Jorvik is like the holy grail. If we can get ties with them, we'll really have arrived. It would have done us more good in the long run."

Her cloak had gold thread in its borders, and was held shut by a silver brooch the size of Billy's fist. He suspected, uncharitably, that she'd simply never experienced what it was like to be in want. You could only afford to think it wasn't about the money when you had enough of the stuff.

Taking a deep breath through his nose and letting it out, he felt some tension leave him. The ground was pleasantly cool beneath him, and he considered toppling over sideways and pressing his cheek to it, closing his eyes.

"You're not fooling us, you know." Rolf's voice interrupted the slow reintegration of Billy's calm. He didn't like the tone of it—hostile, accusatory. It arrested Billy's sideways slump, made him sit up again, braced for fight or flight.

"I don't know what you mean." Martin attempted a laugh that sounded unbearably fake in Billy's ears. Billy's heart rate picked up and the muscles of his flanks shuddered. "I'm not up to something. I haven't got some kind of hidden agenda—"

"Yeah." Rolf had replaced his helmet with a crocheted hat that still failed to make him look any less the hard man of the group. "Of course not. Of course we just keep turning up at events where your morris buddies are also performing out of pure fucking coincidence. And it's pure fucking coincidence that you've got half of us poncing about doing talks about *dancing* instead of concentrating on the battlefield. It's pure fucking coincidence that you spend more time with that prancing nancy of theirs than you do paying attention to us?"

Billy froze as if hit with a freeze ray, trying not even to breathe. Although he generally loathed being invisible, the trait had its advantages. He hoped, painfully, that Martin would not let "prancing nancy" slide—hoped to be defended in his absence, but the hope coexisted with a sickening foreknowledge that it wasn't going to happen.

"Yeah." Martin freed both hands from his cloak so he could spread them wide in a shrug. "Yeah, I've been booking us into things that the Griffins are doing too. What's wrong with that? Most of our bookings this year come from me stealing contacts from their programme. You think we'd have had half these shows without them? They're established, we're new. We're tagging on to their coattails while we build a reputation of our own. We should be thanking them for that."

"You do seem to be spending an awful lot of time with this Early Dance Group." Edith picked up Rolf's complaint and ran with it. "And we need you here. Clients are getting confused as to which group you belong to and—"

"It's *interesting*." Martin withdrew his placatory gesture. A note of implacability entered his voice. "This is a hobby, right? Something I do because I want to. If I want to take it in a new direction, that's up to me."

He sat up straighter, returning accusation for accusation. "I don't have to devote every moment of my life to this society if I don't want to. It's already made me lose my job, what more do you want? You don't think I'm pulling my weight? I'm here every event, I bring the stuff, I set up for everyone, I take the stuff down and take it away. I deal with membership and money for food and organizing the firewood and the water. I get us bookings. If I want to do something else as well, that's none of your fucking business."

Implacable had sledged downhill straight into anger. "If you think I'm taking too much on because I'm researching stuff that fits into our remit and our time period, because it fucking interests me, then maybe some of you should step up to the mark and take some responsibility yourself, instead of leaving it all to me. I wouldn't have to do every bloody thing if you lot would pull your weight. Because, let me tell you, it's been a hell of a long time since any of this was fun for me."

A silence. Billy thought they were abashed as he was. He hadn't thought that he was creating trouble for Martin. That their little venture together might be eroding the things Martin cared about. Why hadn't he thought that he was demanding too much? That there was a cost to Martin in keeping Billy safe, and the cost was too high. *Why must you always do this? Always be so needy and so fucking selfish?* His throat closed and his breathing tightened up again, a giant's hand tight around his rib cage.

Kayleigh laughed, flourishing her bottle of cider so that it gleamed like a citrine in the light of the fire. "Stop giving him a hard time, you lot. He's in luurve. Him and that Billy bloke. *Course* they want to be together. You seriously haven't seen it? It couldn't be more obvious."

Billy tried to pretend he wasn't merely invisible, he was actually not there at all. He wished hard to stop existing, and it only made him hate himself more when he couldn't make the wish come true.

Uncertainty passed like a whisper around the fire, as one by one the Vikings took on the frozen expressions of people who are entertaining a completely unfamiliar thought for the first time.

"Seriously?" said Rolf at last, his voice hovering between discomfort and laughter, as if not quite sure whether Kayleigh was pulling his leg or not. He turned to Martin. "Seriously, you've got a *boyfriend*?"

Martin looked from face to face anxiously, as if for signs that anybody had got his back. Maybe he didn't get them, or maybe he was just so ashamed of Billy he wouldn't have said anything if he had. "He's just a friend. I'm allowed to have friends, aren't I?"

He ground his beer can into the soft sand at the edge of the firebox and stood up, pulling his cloak tighter around himself. One long wine-coloured cylinder with head and feet. "I'm going to bed."

"Martin," Edith said, as if she was working up to something very reasonable. "Don't—"

"Good night." Martin strode away, and while they were all watching his departing form, Billy slipped back out of the gap in the shelter and took refuge in the night.

He wanted to fall to his knees, put his forehead on the cool ground, and let everything go—simply to stop existing until this moment was past, until he had regained some resilience, enough energy to order his thoughts. But he couldn't. There were still people walking up and down the paths through the fairground. People would see it and think he was crazy, and then they would interfere. Then he'd have to talk and manage concerned strangers, interact and form words and make decisions. He didn't have the wherewithal to cope with any of that at the moment.

So he'd thought he could cope with being denied, and it turned out he couldn't. God, he needed Martin right now, needed him like he needed a safe place to curl up in. But Martin *wasn't* safe. Martin didn't want him, couldn't be trusted. Martin colluded with the whole world to make Billy invisible, and he . . . and he . . . maybe he always would. Billy had known that, but he hadn't truly felt it till now. He'd had energy and optimism holding it away. That was gone.

Maybe all those people's opinions would always matter to Martin more than Billy did. And maybe that was all Billy deserved, but even so he wasn't going to fucking stand for it.

He loved Martin. He did. He did. But he was not, *not* something to be ashamed of.

Fuck the bastard. Fuck him.

His plan to stay overnight here was thoroughly screwed. The barrier between himself and Martin's tent, fifty yards away, could not have been more impenetrable if it had been some kind of force field. It offered no real refuge at all, only pretence. He couldn't possibly turn up now and ask for a place to sleep. He had more pride than that, and Martin wouldn't thank him for it.

That left his flat. Thirty miles away, thirty-five maybe. And the Griffins danced here often. He knew the way. The need for home, a refuge, familiarity and a locked door between him and the world took the place of a decision. Willpower and higher thought were both offline—he couldn't think about buses or taxis or train timetables. That was too complicated, too impossible to deal with. He went on instinct and started walking.

CHAPTER TWENTY

The next morning, Martin was still angry, itchy with it beneath the skin. He packed up the group's work shelter, disassembled the firebox, put the sand back into its sandbags and the tent into its cover, and folded up the furs and blankets that lined his floor in lieu of a groundsheet.

The garrison were all noticeably helpful and cheerful towards him.

"Let me get that." Edith lifted the chest of crockery into the trailer as Rolf strapped the tent supports to the roof rack. Martin thought he should lose his rag more often with them if this was the result, but frankly he'd rather have had them take him for granted again, if it came without the memory of being forced to choose between Bretwalda and Billy.

He was pretty sure he'd made the wrong choice.

He'd just panicked. Anyone would have done when put on the spot like that. Anyone would have said whatever they needed to say to get the intrusive personal questions to stop.

Anyone might have done, but he still felt like a shit about it. Thank God Billy had gone home an hour before and hadn't been around to hear it, because if it was making him feel like this, what would it do to someone as fine tuned, as sensitive as Billy?

He slung his chain mail and shield on top of the deflated air bed in the boot and wedged his three spears down the side of the car, in the gap between the seats and the doors.

"So, we'll see you at Detling?" Rolf rubbed one hand across the stubble of his hair, beneath which the Odin rune tattooed on his head gleamed blue. He had the other hand thrust deep in his pocket. His shoulders were hunched, and Martin could tell perfectly well that this was an apology and a request for forgiveness. He just wasn't feeling very forgiving at the moment. What was the point of them leaving their old society if they were only going to reestablish the bitching in this one?

"Maybe." He got into the car, closed the door, rolled down the window, and relented a little. "If I can't make it, I'll make sure someone picks up the kit and brings it down for you."

Rolf rocked onto his back foot, opened his mouth, and then closed it again as he decided to settle for what he could get. "Yeah, okay. See you, then."

Martin drove away, and everyone in Bretwalda waved at him as he went. Bad news travelled fast, apparently, if everyone knew they had to be nice to him this morning.

At home, he unloaded the tent and the work shelter, spreading the canvas out in the living room among the litter of craft projects, the half-made leather cups, the woodworking tools, the disassembled shaving horse propped against the end of the sofa. There had been rain in the middle of the night, and the tent would need to dry for a couple of days before he could put it away properly.

He brought in the cooking equipment and the trestle tables, the bouquet of antlers, the basket full of nets, the hides and wicker eel-pots, the sieve, the bellows, the tripod and its chain. The crockery that needed to be washed before it could be shoved back behind the door and forgotten.

It was nine in the evening before he'd finished, and he was still angry. Where did they get off telling him he wasn't allowed to have other interests? Where did they get off looking at him like that, laughing like that, as if it was somehow unthinkable that he might be gay? Why? Because he was black, and everyone knew there were no gay black men? Or was it just because they couldn't believe anyone they actually knew could play for the other team?

Wankers.

He peeled out of his Viking clothes, packed them away without washing them. Washing damaged the dye and fatigued the material, and the smell of deep-ingrained sweat and smoke was far more authentic than that of laundry detergent. Then he went into the bathroom and set about trying to bring himself back to the twenty-first century.

He caught sight of his braids in the mirror before it steamed, and they pissed him off. Time for a change. He hacked them off with the kitchen scissors, unwound the remnants, leaving himself with short unkempt curls. It felt good to be without the weight of them, good to be able to get his fingers in and work shea butter through what was left, soothe his tender scalp. His hair follicles ached to the touch.

Once he was dried and dressed, he ate a packet of Super Noodles with a tin of sweetcorn stirred into it and wondered if now was a good time to call Billy. Phone in his hand, he slouched back out to the car, the anger finally loosening its grip, his head feeling oddly unanchored. Could he cope with getting back on the road and driving for another hour?

The hand of the petrol gauge was hovering just above red. If he did go, he'd have to fill up again, and he couldn't really afford that. He thought of Billy's flat, a second home by now, with his toothbrush in the holder and a set of his clothes in the drawers, and wondered how you asked someone who clearly needed his privacy to function if you could maybe ... perhaps ... *please* move in.

If he did, he'd have to tell everyone. Scratch that—everyone would know even if he didn't tell them. But he'd still have the Early Dance Group. Annette already knew. And Bretwalda's anxious contrition this morning *might* mean he wouldn't lose them either. Not all of them, at least.

He was getting tired of pretending, to be honest. There was something rather pleasing about the thought of letting people know that he'd caught a gorgeous thing like Billy. The thought of coming out was terrifying, but he didn't have any real doubt that he ought to get it done. He didn't have anything to be ashamed of, after all, and if he lost jobs or reenactors or his father over it, then those things would not have been worth keeping anyway.

Can I see you tomorrow? he texted Billy and went back indoors to turn the computer on so that they could at least Skype before going to bed.

Billy's Skype came up unavailable, which wasn't like him. He generally put the computer on first thing in the morning and often forgot to switch it off at all. Martin put a Star Trek movie on to play in the background and tried to relax, but after half an hour with no reply to his text, he gave in and phoned.

"Hello. This is Billy Wright's answering machine. If you have something to say to me, speak and I'll listen."

Martin turned the volume of the TV down as Kirk hung off something by his fingernails. "Um, hi, it's me. Martin. Are you okay? If you're off doing something interesting, then that's great, but I know you crash sometimes after a dance out, so if you can call me back, please do. I just want to be sure you're all right."

He spotted the message light blinking on his landline answerphone as he was passing through the hall eating toast, leading him to drop a slice butter side down on the floor. Billy?

"Hello?" He wedged the phone between his ear and shoulder and retrieved the toast, now covered in bits of grass and an earwig that had come in with the canvas.

It was not Billy. It was St. Dunstan's Church of England (Aided) School who had called on Friday afternoon to tell him that they were sorry but he hadn't quite impressed them enough at the interview stage and they would not be giving him a job.

He sulked about that for a good half hour as he toasted the heel of the loaf and ate it. His pride had led him astray, and no amount of rationing was going to stretch his savings any further. He had kept putting it off, but now it really was time to bow to the inevitable and go sign on for Jobseeker's Allowance, which would at least presumably allow him to eat, though there wouldn't be anything left over to pay the bills.

He emailed off a few more job applications and tried not to think about it too hard. Billy couldn't know somehow, could he? He couldn't know that Martin had denied their relationship in front of his whole society? No, of course he couldn't. He hadn't been there. It was just Martin's guilty conscience tormenting him, and Billy was blissfully ignorant. He was fine.

Of course he was. He was probably just in the grip of a particularly bad down. He must have gone to bed as soon as he got home and stayed there. If so, pestering him would only make him worse. Martin should go to sleep himself and try again in the morning, when they would both be feeling better. So he switched everything off and turned in, spent four hours trying to calm down enough to fall asleep and only managed it just as the sun was coming up.

Having fallen asleep at five, he didn't wake until midmorning, when the phone rang. *Thank God*, he thought, picking it up so sharply that he bashed his jaw with his own knuckles. "Billy?"

"No, it's Nicky Riley from English Heritage, Mr. Deng. We met at Dover Castle?"

Martin rubbed a hand through his hair and let the bruised feeling of his scalp distract him from a worry that was building into something volcanic by now. "I remember. Sorry. Go ahead."

"I've got some good news for you," she said, seemingly amused by his incompetence. "We've had an enquiry from a Mr. Inman, who was in the crowd that day. He's a producer for the BBC, and he wants to talk to you about possibly doing some film work. I understand he's doing a fantasy series set in the Dark Ages and wants some authentic-looking extras with their own kit. I said I would pass along his number and you would phone him to talk further."

"Absolutely." Martin tried to sound as enthusiastic about this as it deserved, his mind working on the problem of how to get the guy to feature the Early Dance Group in more than one episode. "But the group is really more Billy Wright's baby. He might be the person to do it?"

"I understand that," she said dismissively, "but he's not answering his phone this morning and you are. So here is Mr. Inman's number, and I'll leave the rest up to you."

Martin wrote the number down, feeling a little sick. Okay, so it wasn't just that Billy was avoiding him for some reason. He was either avoiding *everyone* or something even more sinister was happening.

At the thought of "sinister," Kaminski's face came to mind, along with the police in the hallway downstairs, with their professionally closed faces that gave nothing away. *Don't be ridiculous. People don't get kidnapped or blown up by Russian mafia mobsters in real life. That kind of thing only happens in films.*

Except it didn't. If there was some kind of Eastern European terrorist cell at work in Billy's ground-floor flat, you could bet all the neighbours would say, *We were so surprised. That sort of thing doesn't happen here.* And yet if it happened at all, it had to happen somewhere, to people someone knew. What if this time those people were Billy and him?

You're being paranoid.

Maybe, but then why *were* the police there?

Martin dragged the paperwork for his car insurance and his breakdown cover renewal out of the pile of "urgent things to be paid when I can afford them," and thought that maybe he could manage one of them *if* he used the petrol money on it. That still added up to no way of actually going physically to Billy's place and checking on him.

Could he phone one of the garrison and ask for a lift, after he'd just pissed them all off over this very issue? They'd know, if he did, that his "we're just friends" thing was the bullshit it was.

Why not? Kill two birds with one stone. Rip the plaster off the coming-out thing with one movement while more important things were taking up his mind. If they didn't like it, they could take their judgement and stick it. This was no time to be worrying about something so trivial.

He was scrolling through his contacts, trying to remember who lived closest to him, when the phone buzzed again in his hand. "Hello?"

"Hi, Martin? It's Annette."

His heart did a good impression of a black hole at the sound of her voice, the uncertainty, the concern. "Hi."

"Um, is Billy there with you? I wouldn't normally ask, but he didn't come to practice last night."

"Is that so unusual? He'd had a full day of dancing the day before. Maybe he was tired?"

"No." He could hear his own anxiety reflected in her tightening tone. "No, you don't understand. He never misses practice. That's why we call him 'Constant Billy.' Because in five years I've never known him to miss a practice once. I called his house, but he's not answering, and his mobile's turned off. Did something happen?"

"Nothing I know of. Not between us, anyway. You sure it's not a slightly-worse-than-usual crash? Maybe he's lying on the sofa ignoring the world."

"He wouldn't miss practice," she insisted. "It's one of the things he does to manage his condition—structure his life, you know, so that he doesn't have to make too many decisions."

Martin put a hand over his eyes and massaged his temples while his worry shook the earth beneath him. "Shit. Can you go round there?"

"I did," she said heavily. "Straight after practice last night, and then again first thing this morning. No one's answering the door, but I'm sure I heard someone moving around in that ground-floor flat. He was watching me as I left, that lodger of Billy's. Peering through the letter box, the ridiculous man."

CHAPTER
TWENTY-ONE

Shit. Shit. The closest member of Bretwalda to Martin's house lived an hour's drive away, and probably wouldn't come anyway. He thumbed the phone off, got his keys, and ran to the car. Thanks to far too many gangster movies, he kept having vivid flashes of imagination—Billy tied up somewhere with cable ties, gagged and helpless, bundled into a cupboard or under the stairs. That wouldn't be so bad. Martin could get him out, and they could both recover from that.

Billy already dead with a bullet through his brain, shoved in a cocoon of bin bags with bricks to make him sink, thrown into one of the county's many canals. That one was not such a good thought. He tried to avoid having that one as he accelerated up the road, cursing all the cautious drivers ahead of him who kept maliciously slowing him down.

He tried to avoid that thought. But it kept coming back.

Halfway to Billy's house, just passing the odd sail-shaped roof of the Castleton Outdoors Centre, the car coughed under him as though something had tried to trip it up. Martin's heart hit him in the roof of his mouth. *What?*

The sensation passed. He drove on another mile, hoping, hoping it wouldn't come again. And then it did. Twice. He slowed, forced to accept that yes, this was happening, there really was something wrong. What the hell? How could this be his life?

The realization came like falling flat on his face from horseback. No, God! Don't say he'd . . .

With a final jerk and shudder, the engine stalled, and he coasted to the side of the road where he could tuck the useless vehicle into a lay-by. The arrow of the petrol gauge now pointed below the red, as if it had sunk through the floor. He'd been so preoccupied with getting there quickly, he'd forgotten to fill up.

Fuck! Fuck! He got out, slammed his hand against the door arch, hurt his palm, and swore at the machine for a good minute and a half, ending up bent forward, head down, and stymied. Life had brought him to a stop. He didn't know what to do next. Couldn't phone for a breakdown recovery—the cover had lapsed—couldn't help Billy from here. Couldn't come to the rescue like he had promised himself he would.

Looking back, he couldn't put his finger on the point where this desperate need to protect Billy had flowered into one of the mainstays of his life, but wasn't it just like his life that he should recognise it now, when there was nothing at all he could do?

Leaning against the useless car, he put his head in his hands while he thought. Okay, he could still phone Rolf. Rolf lived three hours away, but judging from his shame-faced look yesterday he'd be glad of the opportunity to do Martin a favour.

Martin tried to breathe until his tight throat had loosened enough to speak, but every time he tried to straighten up the ball in his chest pulled him back down. He couldn't even stand up now. Turning, he put his back to the car and slid down to sit on the tarmac, surprised that the air above him could feel so heavy.

The sound of a distant motorbike reached him as he paged again through his contacts, trying to find Rolf's number. The day was wet and cool around him, and the tarmac beneath him was cold. Bluish vegetables grew in the fields that lined the road on either side, and he just knew he was going to hate the smell of leeks forever after this. He lowered his gaze back to the foot of tarmac immediately in front of him and hit Call.

The phone had just begun to ring when a wheel and a foot came into his view, the foot clad in a high-tech, white-and-silver motorcycle boot.

"You need any help down there?"

Martin looked up and saw an angel. Or possibly a Hell's Granny. The woman was clearly over sixty, her eyes white-ringed beneath heavy glasses, her white-and-silver helmet matching her hair. She rode a silver Norton Commando and was decked out in white-and-silver leathers.

Perhaps on another occasion he might have thoughtlessly mocked this attempt to achieve in old age what she had clearly missed out on in her youth. Right now, Martin couldn't think of a vision of more loveliness.

"I think my friend's in trouble, and I can't... The car is..."

"I could take you." She interrupted his struggle for words with calm. "Our main problem is the helmet. I don't carry a spare."

Martin's paralysis passed like a storm cloud. He tore to his feet. "I can do that. I can do that!" Thank God for his laziness—he had unpacked the car of those things that needed to be dealt with, the perishable things, the things that didn't like to sit in their own damp and go mouldy. But he'd left, at the back of the boot, all of his armour and his shields. He opened the boot up, fished inside, and brought out the spangenhelm, which gleamed dull and sinister against the rain-dark sky.

"Oh!" The woman's helmet already gave her a chipmunk-cheeked look. Her smile only made it worse. "I say! I always used to dream of being stolen away by a handsome Viking. Better late than never, eh?" She held out a hand to shake, as Martin tightened the strap of his helmet beneath his chin. "I'm Laurie. Pleased to meet you. Where are we going?"

"Martin." He grinned, shaking her hand. "You are a lifesaver. Possibly literally. Can you take me to 12 High Street, Rosebery Wood, as quickly as possible, please?"

She was old, and old people, notoriously, tended to have older opinions. He briefly considered lying again and couldn't face it. He'd shamed himself enough in front of Bretwalda. It was time to be brave. The words were hard to get out, but they were the only ones that would come. "I think my boyfriend's in trouble. I need to get there fast."

The rain had blown away when they drew up in Rosebery Wood, and the sun was making the wet world as silver as Laurie's rig. Billy's house looked impossibly picturesque, with its blue front door and the tubs of marigolds and geraniums that lined the stone steps up to it.

"It doesn't look like the scene of a crime," said Laurie as Martin climbed stiffly from the pillion of her bike. "But good luck anyway. I hope it goes well." She waved a parting salute, which he answered halfheartedly, and roared away as he contemplated the shut door and the darkness behind the windows.

Unlacing his helmet, he tore up the steps two at a time and hammered on the door. "Billy? Billy, are you in there? It's me, Martin."

As Annette had implied, there was something eerie about the silence that followed. His instincts told him it was not an empty silence but a silence in which some listener was trying hard to be quiet. It stretched unbearably. He waited, impatient and anxious, sure that eventually whoever it was who was hidden behind the door would crack and open it. Sure they would. Sure of it. He was sure...

"Billy!" His body seemed to have reached panic earlier than his mind. He was hitting the door hard with his fist tight in the webbing of his helmet. The thunder of steel on wood echoed down the tiled floor inside and reflected back at him. "If you don't answer me I'm going to get in some other way. I'm going to break a window or knock down the door. Let me in!"

Still nothing. Doves flapped with whistling wings around the bell cote of the church tower. He felt rather than saw a neighbour's net curtains twitch in the house opposite Billy's. He gathered he was ten minutes away from being intercepted and escorted away by a posse of concerned locals. "Fine!"

It didn't look difficult when he saw it on the TV. He turned to one side, took as long a run up as the small paved landing above the steps could provide, and drove his weight through his shoulder directly into the plate of the lock.

The door cracked against its jamb as he rammed it. Agony clawed up his neck and down his arm, lancing through his back and his ribs. *Ah, fuck!* He recoiled. The door bounced back with a clatter and stood smugly undamaged and unopened. Someone came out from the back garden of the house across the street and shouted "Oi!" as Martin yelled with pain and fury, kicked the door viciously, making it boom like a drum.

"What do you think you're—?" began the denim-clad neighbourhood watchman from over the road.

Shit, thought Martin and darted looks from right to left, trying to find somewhere to run.

"Very well. I open." And there was rattling behind Billy's front door. A moment later, it swung slightly inwards, enough for Martin to push through, slam it shut again, and put his back to it, keeping the elderly vigilante out.

He was face-to-face with Kaminski, and the other man's fist-flattened face was not happy at all. They stood, watching one another warily. And yes, Martin was pretty handy with a sword, and could hold his own in a contest with axes, but something about Kaminski's posture, the corded strength in that wiry neck, the flatness of his narrowed eyes, suggested here was a man who did for real what Martin only played at.

"You want what, now?"

Well, okay, perhaps running himself into the same trap had not been the best move, but now he was here, he might as well play the role of rescuing hero to the hilt. "I want to know where Billy Wright is. No one's heard from him for two days. His friends are worried."

"And you think I have what? Abducted him? Because I am Polish, you think, 'He is underworld criminal up to no good'?" Kaminski's eyes narrowed again until they were like little slits of moonstone, cloudy grey and gleaming. "*You* know better, I think."

Martin felt a little abashed. Some of the wired aggression bled out from his fingertips. "I'm sorry," he said, slumping. "But Billy is really missing. Do you know anything about that?"

In response to Martin's semisurrender, Kaminski's fists eased open. He stepped back and turned, holding open the door to his flat. "Come. Come in."

Come into my lair, said the spider to the fly. "Why?"

"No more talking with the door open. You come in, I lock. Then we talk."

"That doesn't sound like such a—"

Kaminski grabbed Martin by the elbow and yanked. Taken by surprise, Martin unbalanced and practically ran into the room while trying to regain his footing. Just as he'd said he would, Kaminski shut the door behind him, locked the three locks with a set of keys he kept in his pocket and slipped shut three heavy bolts. Nothing was getting through that door now.

Feeling suddenly sick, Martin looked to the window, in no way surprised to find it covered with a light metal grille that was screwed into the wood of the frame. *Oh God.* So much for riding to the rescue. Was he about to become the next victim?

The rest of the flat was hardly the den of iniquity he had been fearing. The bare boards of the floor were painted white to match the walls. The minimalist living space was uncluttered, except for a large black leather sofa and a light with a shade made from black-and-white cowhide. A huge black plasma TV was bolted to the wall in front of the sofa. Behind the sofa some reclaimed railway sleepers had been turned into freestanding bookshelves. Behind those, against the supporting wall of the house, stood a locked metal cabinet easily big enough to contain four trussed-up bodies if they were hung on meat hooks, or stiff enough to stand.

Kaminski caught him looking at it, gave a smug, almost gloating smile.

Martin backed towards the door, though he knew there was no getting out of it. Nothing in the room presented itself as a weapon that he could use, but he would need to at least knock the other man out long enough to get the keys out of his pocket. He could feel his heart whining beneath his breastbone like a saw, and when he moved, he could smell the acrid reek of fear on himself, shameful and embarrassing.

"You let me out right now or I—"

Kaminski's smile dropped away. His mouth twisted with something rueful, bitter. "You *are* afraid of me. Why?"

Maybe the lamp, Martin thought. Maybe he could duck behind the sofa, grab the lamp, and use it as a spear. He was bloody good with a spear, and once the shade had been dislodged and the bulb broken, a six-foot wrought iron pole topped with shattered glass should deter anyone. He edged towards it. "Normal people don't get the police round at five o'clock in the morning. Normal people don't have cases full of ammunition, or lock their guests in before they'll talk. Billy's disappeared, and you're freaking me out, so—"

"Normal people do not have guns, this is true." Kaminski interrupted him, his voice soft now and reasonable, with a note of implacability behind it—an army commander bracing up the nerves of a panicking new recruit while reassuring them that he was perfectly in charge of the situation.

Oddly enough it did steady Martin, made him pause in his preparations to fight to the death.

"But I am president of rifle club," Kaminski went on. "I have my guns, and I have spare guns belonging to the club in my house. I must be careful not to let anyone in to steal them, so I lock, always, the door between them and the outside world."

Cold humiliation began to give way to a sear of hot humiliation in Martin's stomach. This sounded so reasonable, so responsible. "And the police?" he asked, relaxing in slow, jerky increments while a wave of nausea passed over him as prickly as pins and needles.

"For my gun licence they must come and inspect. Make sure I keep everything locked in gun cabinet, make sure house is secure. I am sorry they come so early, but I had meeting later in day in London, so it was convenient for me."

"Oh God." Martin dropped his head into his hands and held on tight through the sickness and the dizziness of a great wash of needless adrenaline dissipating through his system. "Oh God, I'm sorry. I'm sorry. I should have guessed it would be something like that. Or asked—we should maybe have just asked."

"Hmm." Kaminski huffed a laugh through his nose. "Is not the first time. I am in army when I am young. Boxing champion. Now my face is not good advertisement for my peaceful nature."

"But, like you say, that kind of thing happens to me too. I should have known better." One final pass to wipe the shame from his face and Martin sighed, straightened up. "*Do* you know where Billy is?"

"He is upstairs." Kaminski waved a hand to indicate the flat above, and Martin breathed in deeply for the first time in days. "I am going out, yesterday evening, and I find him there. Outside my door. I think he is asleep, at first, but no, he is lying on the floor, with his eyes open, not moving."

The brief feeling of relief morphed into horror. "*Yesterday* evening? What happened to the day before that?"

"I did not ask. I pick him up and look—he is not hurt anywhere. When I make him stand, he stands; he does not fall down again. I tell him to walk upstairs; he walks upstairs. But he is very tired, I think. I find keys, unlock door. I tell him to go to bed, he goes to bed. I put water and chocolate next to bed, then I leave. This morning I hear shower running and TV on, so I think he is better and it is no longer my business. This I leave to you."

"Okay." Martin sighed. "Okay, that's on the better end of the things I feared. I can cope with that. Okay, okay, God. That's good."

The relief left him feeling momentarily limp, still leaning on Kaminski's front door, with his eyes closed and his head bent. He gave himself a minute to allow the day's terrors to drain away, to brace himself back up again for action.

"You want a beer?"

Martin laughed. "God, yes! Desperately. But I'd better not. If you let me out, I'll go and make sure he's all right." He moved aside so that Kaminski could go through the lengthy process of unbarring the door. "Thank you for looking after him. I'm Martin, by the way, his boyfriend."

That was considerably easier to say the second time around, and he hoped that Kaminski would understand that he was being told this sensitive information in the trust that he was the kind of man who could treat it properly. He hoped Kaminski would see that this was an apology.

"Jacek." Kaminski put out a large hand with stars tattooed over the knuckles, and they shook to cement a new alliance. Martin ducked through the narrow gap of the door and smiled to have it slammed closed behind him and immediately locked and bolted again. What had seemed a sinister habit now seemed an excess of responsibility, as knowledge turned danger into reassurance.

He looked at the stairs, braced himself again, and then went up, knocking gently on Billy's door at the top. He too could hear the TV from here, the reassuring drone of some documentary.

No one answered the knock, but he knew enough now not to take that personally. He checked the handle, pushed it down. The unlocked door opened for him, and he went in.

CHAPTER TWENTY-TWO

Billy lay on the sofa. The TV was on, but Billy had turned towards the back of the couch, his forehead against the cushions, his eyes closed.

"Billy?" Martin shut the door behind him and edged into the room. There was a full cup of tea on the floor in front of the settee, but when he touched it he found it was cold. The remote lay beside it. It didn't seem likely to Martin that Billy had deliberately tuned the TV to *Hollyoaks*, so he flipped through some channels and found *Poirot* instead. Billy sighed when he turned the programme over, so he was a) not dead, and b) not asleep.

That was good. This was some kind of crash, then, of a deeper, more insidious cast than the ones he had had before. Martin could deal with that. No questions, no pressure. He leaned down to stroke the chocolate-brown curls away from Billy's forehead, which creased in a frown under his palm. "I'm so glad you're okay. I've been so worried."

But no, that was not a conversational tack he could afford to take at this point. He could feel it open up the lids of all the boxes of his own fear and dismay. If he let his own feelings out at this point, they could easily turn to anger, and anger wouldn't help either of them.

Getting up from his crouch by the coffee table, Martin took the cold tea to the kitchen to make a fresh pot. A fine blue fug and a suspicious warmth hung over everything in there. On the cooker, a blackened saucepan made a creaky pinging noise. It was full of what looked like charcoal, the centre of a little galaxy of swirling smoke. The ring under it was bright red, also giving out the tiny distressed sounds of metal that's been too hot for too long.

Martin grabbed a tea towel to shield his hand and switched the cooker off, appalled. At some point this morning Billy must have tried to cook himself porridge, only to go back into the sitting room, sit down, and find himself unable to get up again to switch it off. That settled it, once and for all. Decision made.

When he brought tea and chocolate biscuits back to the sitting room, it was to find that Billy had not moved an inch, so Martin shook him by the shoulder, adding an insistent tug to the action to give the other man the idea. "Sit up."

Billy's eyes squeezed more firmly closed and his mouth hardened, but Martin wasn't having that. He pulled again. "Sit up, come on."

Gracelessly, begrudgingly, Billy swung himself round to face the room and sat, his shoulders hunched, his face concealed by his swinging hair.

"Good," said Martin and picked up one of his hands, pressing the teacup into it. "Here. Drink the tea."

Billy sighed again, a noise half of anger, half despair, as though Martin was asking more from him than he was capable of achieving. As though it was unreasonable to expect him to endure this pressure and swallow fluids at the same time. But he drank and kept it down. Some of Martin's frantic worry eased.

When he had pestered Billy into eating a chocolate biscuit, Billy's eyes opened and strayed to the television, where Poirot was being sent to a health farm on the advice of Miss Lemon. Martin wasn't sure if he was actually seeing it, or just focussing on the most rapidly moving thing in the room, but it was still progress.

He sat next to Billy and took Billy's right hand in his own, rubbing his thumb gently across the knuckles. It took a while, just sitting shoulder to shoulder, knee to knee, companionable, watching David Suchet walk like a penguin through one of Agatha Christie's more improbable whodunits, but eventually Billy's head turned fractionally towards Martin. From the angle of his head, his gaze had settled on their clasped hands.

"What happened?" Martin asked gently.

"I don't . . . I don't know why you're here."

"I'm here because I love you. I was frantic with worry—you disappeared and I couldn't get through to you. Your side have been worrying. You didn't turn up for practice and that wasn't like you. They thought something terrible had happened. So did I. Where were you yesterday? What happened?"

Billy tried to say something, his face creasing with the effort, but it was too much for him. He shook his head and gave up. Martin wanted to shake him, yell at him to buck up, it couldn't be this hard, but he didn't think that would help. Billy was just processing very slowly at the moment and perhaps two questions at once were too much. He tried again.

"Where were you yesterday?"

"Somewhere on the road," Billy slurred. "I was walking home from Hunstanton, but I needed to lie down, a lot. It was farther—farther than I thought. I wasn't . . . I went the wrong way." His eyes filled with tears, and he pulled his legs up onto the sofa cushions, so he could hug himself around the knees. "I think I got lost. It took so long. I didn't know which way to go."

Martin launched himself to his feet, his own distress coming out the only way it could. When he pulled his hand away from Billy's, Billy flinched, tucked himself in tighter.

"You *walked* home? I thought you went on the minibus, with the rest of your side?"

"I wanted to see you." Billy's voice was flat, unmodulated, all the more desolate for it. "So I stayed. In the dark. I'm sorry."

Martin's mind swung with sickening speed back to the disastrous conversation with Rolf. Could Billy have been there? Outside the ring of firelight, in his black coat and his black-and-blood-red face, if he had kept those bright clear eyes of his averted, he would have been all but invisible.

Shit. Shit. Martin had mentally cast himself in the role of rescuer, champion, healer, and nurse, but this was much worse. He was actually present in the role of bastard, villain—the one who had caused this meltdown with his own cowardice in the first place. "Shit," he said, and clutched at his newly shorn hair, while he fell face-first into a morass of guilt.

"I'm sorry." Billy apologised a second time for being devastated, let down, rejected, and denied. "I didn't want to cause you trouble. I understand you don't want to see me anymore, and I won't make things hard for you. I'm sorry I've done—" he waved a hand towards himself and then towards the kitchen, as if to indicate his current nonfunctioning state "—this. It wasn't to make you feel bad. You weren't supposed to see. I don't understand what you're doing here."

Billy turned sideways, trying to hide himself in the cushions, defend himself from the pressures of a world that was too much for him, and Martin couldn't bear to watch it. He sat down abruptly, drew Billy into his arms, and pressed Billy's face instead into the hollow of his shoulder. Here was a better shelter. Here was someone who would do more than just passively shield him. *I will stand between you and everything*, he thought, his chest aching with the knowledge that that would never be possible. That all he could offer would not be enough.

Hard on the heels of that thought came the knowledge that Billy had trusted him to do that very thing, and he had royally fucked it up like the utter coward he was. He wanted to curl himself into Billy and hold on, drowned under his own regrets, but that at least he would not do. One of them had to pick them both up, mend all of this, and it was only right that it should be him.

"I'm sorry," Billy muttered again, the sound of it muffled by Martin's shirt.

"Don't apologise to me!"

"I'm sorry."

Martin did give way to the desire to shake Billy, just gently, at that. "No, please," he begged, with his eyes watering, having to fight with his own body to get the words out. He had never understood better what Billy felt like during these episodes of his—it was like he was clinging by his nails to the edge of an abyss. "I'm the one who's sorry. I didn't mean what I said to Rolf—what I said to all of them. I was being a coward. I didn't mean it."

He breathed carefully, trying to slow down his heartbeat, to keep his voice soft and soothing, but he couldn't help the words coming faster, tripping over each other in their haste to be said.

"If you'll take me back, there'll be no more hiding, I promise. I promise. Oh God, Billy, I'm so sorry. I want you to know I would never have said anything like that if I'd known you were listening. That doesn't make it any better, does it? But I mean, I would never have hurt you like that intentionally. I didn't mean to. I know that doesn't make a lot of—"

Billy tried to curl away from him, hearing the anger, the accusation in his tone. Martin was only angry with himself, but that was too complicated for Billy to understand right now. He heard anger, he must have believed it was anger at him. Martin's fear, love, and contrition didn't seem to be getting through at all.

Billy's lip wobbled and fresh tears dampened Martin's neck. "I'm sorry!"

"Hey, hey, hey . . ." Now Martin was crying too, in sympathy and guilt. What a horrific thing this was that Billy was battling. How all encompassing and how poisonous. It pressed between them like a wall, stopping Billy from hearing Martin's concern, blocking Martin's love from passing through, from doing any good.

It occurred to him suddenly, catastrophically, that he might lose Billy over this, and the tearing, floor-opening pain of that put all his fears over his father and everything else into perspective. *God, please no. Anything but that.*

But he didn't deserve to have his feelings considered right now—didn't deserve to panic and beg Billy for a forgiveness that was a huge decision. Billy was currently not capable of deciding to switch the oven off before the house caught on fire. Forcing him to think about whether or not to forgive Martin right now seemed unfair.

Martin tried again for calm reassurance, for a kind of solidity where Billy could find his feet. "You've done nothing wrong. Nothing at all. I love you. You are the most beautiful, most talented person I've ever met. I think you're wonderful, and I want to stay with you forever."

No reaction, positive or negative. He couldn't even be sure Billy was still listening. He felt like a cartoon character, run out over a deadly drop, his legs still pinwheeling, but he couldn't stop running for fear he would fall.

"I know I've been a shit," he admitted. "I know how it's bothered you for a long time, and every bloody time I went my own way and pleased myself and didn't think about what you wanted. It's not like that was the only time I disappointed you. It was just the worst. But, Billy, it was also the last, I promise you that.

"I want to tell everyone we're together. I want everyone to know, and if they don't like it, then fuck them all, right? As long as I've got you. But I don't ever want you to have to go through this again. You're never coming home to an empty flat where you lie here helpless, not even drinking while you set the place on fire around you because no one's here to look after you. It's not happening again, do you hear me? If Dad tells me he never wants to speak to me again, if I never get another job, that's fine. You're what's important. I've seen that now. I promise. I promise you, Billy. I love you, and I always will."

Billy made a strangled, disbelieving noise and clutched so tight at Martin's shirt that he could hear the seams creak with the strain. Scrambling up into his lap, all long coltish legs and spidery arms, Billy wrapped himself tight around Martin, his face still buried in Martin's neck. Moving under his own power. That was an improvement. Martin managed a watery smile and leaned back into the cushions, running his hands reassuringly up and down Billy's back, feeling the rigid muscles begin to soften and shake.

Slowly, beneath the reassuring caress, Billy turned heavy again, sagged into Martin's embrace until he was lying as lax as a sleeping child over Martin's supporting frame. "I'm sorry," he said at last, his voice washed out, drowsy, but without the undertones of frantic despair it had carried earlier. A voice of reason. "I don't like to be made invisible."

You don't like to be visible either, Martin thought ruefully. But that might well be true of both of them. Why else would they have both chosen to spend their every leisure moment pretending to be someone else?

"I know," he said. "I know. I went away, and I felt like such a bastard because I know I should have told the truth to them, and I especially should have been proud. I *am* proud that you're with me, Billy. It's not going to happen again, I promise you. We are official now, you and I. I am going to tell Bretwalda at the next show, and if they don't like it, they can go fuck themselves."

"Really?"

"Really really." Martin sniffed back his own tears. "And I'm going to hold your hand when we're out on the street. And if anyone objects, I'm going to set my army on them."

Billy huffed a tired little laugh at that into the bare skin of Martin's neck. It made him warm all over.

"Yeah? Even though I'm . . ." Billy half raised a hand and let it fall. "I'm like this? Even though I'm so . . . *useless* and—"

"You're not useless," Martin said firmly, beginning to tremble with relief. It almost looked as though the crisis had been averted, although the situation was still not exactly normal. He couldn't be sure if he had been forgiven, but Billy seemed to be recovering, and his own uncertainty was unimportant beside that. "But you are really tired, springbok, aren't you? Do you want to go to bed?"

The thinning clouds darkened again. "I don't know!" Billy growled, upset.

Martin shoved them both upright. As Kaminski had said, Billy was stable enough once he was up—it was not his body that was to blame for any of this. But clearly he'd been expecting too much to ask for a decision, even one so easy as sleep versus no sleep.

He got them all the way to the bedroom. The glass of water Kaminski had mentioned was still there on the side table, still full, so he lowered Billy to a sitting position on the side of the bed, told him to drink it, and watched to make sure. Tomorrow he was going to make a doctor's appointment and take Billy to it. Because yes, he loved the guy even when he was a surly, weepy mess on the sofa, but it hurt to see Billy in such misery. Surely there had to be some kind of medicine for this? This whole disaster could have been so much worse, but that didn't mean he wanted anything like it to ever happen again.

Billy had only managed to pull on pyjama bottoms after his shower, so it was easy to roll him into the duvet. Martin unzipped his own jeans and unbuttoned his shirt, catching sight of his paperback on his own side of the bed, the sock he thought he'd lost poking out of the top of the laundry basket. He stripped to his boxers and slid in next to Billy, gathering him in his arms. Billy was still quiet, withdrawn, but he curled like a small animal into Martin's warmth, so trusting and needy that Martin was charmed all over again.

This is not the time to force him to make decisions, he thought, and pressed a tender kiss on the nape of Billy's neck. *But nor is it the time to leave him alone.* "I'm going to be moving in," he said, slow so that Billy could object if he wanted to, but sure so that Billy need not marshal himself to ask. "I'm going to take you to the doctor tomorrow. In a couple of days we're going to be TV stars. Then in a fortnight at the Cambridge show I'm going to tell everyone in Bretwalda we're together. How does that sound for a plan?"

Billy huffed again and turned to hook both arms around Martin's shoulders, to rest his head back in what was obviously the place that had been designed for it between Martin's shoulder and his neck. "Mmm," he said. "Okay."

Thank God, Martin thought, almost impatient for it now. Impatient to prove he was worthy of being forgiven. *Thank God.*

CHAPTER TWENTY-THREE

"The idea was that you bring your own props."

Billy spread his new yellow cloak out over the industrial space heater in the corner of the film set. The cannon-sized device was busily churning out a steady flow of hot air into the hangar-like space of the set. Ten minutes on there and his soaked clothes would be dry.

He peeled Annette's over-dress off the machine and took it back to her, watching her draw it on at once and huddle in the current of warmth.

"These are not 'props.'" Martin stood a little away from the rest of them, locked in a polite but vital battle with the set director. "These are real musical instruments, and they will be ruined if we take them out there again."

Billy put his own over-tunic on the heater and carefully moved the hearpe a foot closer to the source of warmth. He liked the tone of passionate conviction in Martin's voice. It made him feel cared for.

He'd been feeling that a lot since Martin woke him to breakfast, dragged him to the doctors, and spoke for him when the questions were too hard for him to answer. He had no medicine yet, but blood tests and further appointments to discuss them were on the cards, and he had no doubt Martin would help him remember those too, and get to them.

Just that thought had helped. The thought that from now on he didn't have to do it alone. And Martin's confession, the knowledge that he never wanted to deny Billy's importance to him again, that had helped too.

Billy was still low—huddling here on the pretext of getting warm rather than taking on the producers for himself—but he felt hopeful for the first time that this might be a low he could climb out of and then fill in behind him so he never fell so far again.

"You can't see the instruments properly anyway," Martin was saying now, gesturing at the small screen playing back their last cut. "We could knock up some rough props and then record the music later in a properly dry, temperature-controlled studio."

"He's starting to sound like a musician, isn't he?" Annette sank gracefully to the concrete floor, where the space heater's blast blew back her wimple and made her gown flutter picturesquely. She tugged her kantele a little further into the warmth too.

"I'm sorry about this," Billy said quietly. "They didn't mention anything about getting wet."

Christine returned from the refreshments van with hot chocolates and Eccles cakes for all. "They feed you well, though."

"I suppose."

The Early Dance Group had spent five hours in this big concrete box of a room. Green screens hung from every wall, but the floor contained a massive tank full of water and a wave machine. For some reason, the story, about which the film crew seemed extremely cagy, required the heroes to be shipwrecked, to have built a raft, and to be drifting, delirious with thirst, through the stormy ocean.

Then—when they were just about to give up hope, of course—they would hear distant, eerie music and catch a glimpse, through the rain, of dancing figures on a mysterious island. But when they struggled to shore to beg for help, the dancers would be nowhere to be seen.

So far so good. They'd spent from nine till one in front of the green screens while various polystyrene rocks and trees were arranged around them to the director's satisfaction. A choreographer had worked with Martin and Billy to change the dances to something a bit more photogenic, and they had run through several rehearsals until they were consistently hitting the same marks.

It had been fun, right up until the film crew turned the overhead hoses on to create a more believable rainstorm. Pelting, icy rain had soaked their hair and their clothes, sapping any body heat that had managed to survive the air conditioning. But more seriously, water had got on the thin flexible wood of the stringed instruments, threatening to make it swell and warp, threatening to ruin them.

While the musicians didn't mind roughing it too much for themselves, cruelty to their instruments was another matter. They had come off to dry the hearpe and kantele and absolutely refused to go back on.

"I'll see what I can do," said the unit director to Martin, summoning a minion. Martin watched him go and came back to sit with the rest of the group in their tired and cold huddle around the heater.

"I'm sorry," Martin said, "I thought this would be more glamorous."

"Not a problem." Matt smiled at Martin and then at Billy. "I hear congratulations are in order?"

Billy stiffened, caught in the spotlight of the group's attention, feeling the rare sensation of being very visible indeed. What would Martin say? This, this was his first chance to get it right. Would he flub it?

Martin too looked as pinned as a butterfly against a board. He visibly braced himself, swallowing. "Well, I'm not sure."

Billy frowned.

"I mean, Billy and I just moved in together. I'm not sure if that warrants congratulations."

A deep breath, and when he sighed it out, Billy could feel a profound oppression flowing out of him. Martin had meant it. He had said he would stop being ashamed, and he was speaking the truth.

"You're . . . together?" Christine looked between the two of them with bright birdlike movements, evidently not sure she was putting the pieces together right.

"Oh, Chris." Annette got to her feet. "Were you the last to know?"

She enveloped Billy and then Martin in a slightly damp hug, and asked the important question. "So, Martin, when are you joining the Griffins?"

Billy laughed aloud. He saw Martin's face light up with joy at the sound, and then he was being hugged. Hugged, in public, lifted around the waist and swung. His laugh caught on itself and became a happiness so poignant it felt like anguish. He held on tight and told himself that now he never had to let go.

He hadn't expected this. Finn had told him to fight, but fighting for his own rights was not Billy's thing. If anything, he had expected that such a severe crash, the knowledge that he was dangerous to himself and to others, would have driven Martin away altogether. He still couldn't believe the man could possibly love the spineless wet jellyfish mess that was him.

But he must, mustn't he? He had seen how much pain his denial had caused Billy—he had seen Billy's feelings clear all the way through—and that had been enough to change him. He wasn't someone against whom Billy *had to* fight, and Billy was so grateful, so incredibly grateful for that. Clearly he had meant all those anguished, passionate things he had said. For some unfathomable reason, he must love Billy. Probably the only man in the world who could.

"All right, then." The unit director had reappeared. Martin put Billy down with a slight wince that Billy forgave when he made no attempt to drop Billy's hand.

One of the crew handed Billy an oval lump of wood with a hole cut out of it and strings nailed over the hole. A second triangular plank went to Annette. "The props department knocked these up. We'll record the music separately in the studio as you suggested. Incidentally, the costumes are looking good on the rushes. Very believable. If you have more contacts, we could do with twenty warriors for a tavern fight scene in three weeks. Ever since Lord of the Rings made us all look bad, you just can't get away with the knitted chain mail anymore."

"That would be brilliant." Martin beamed. "My other society, Bretwalda, would be more than happy to provide up to thirty fully kitted warriors if you need them."

He looked at Billy, and his smile fell, obviously remembering that he hadn't told Bretwalda yet. That he didn't know how they would react. That he didn't know if he would still have authority to make any decision for them in three weeks' time.

"At least, I think they would. I have a few issues that need discussing with them first."

Billy pushed back his damp hair with a cold hand, leaned his forehead against his palm, and refused to feel guilty. Absolutely refused.

Martin had begun to move things into Billy's flat—a chest of drawers by the side of the bed full of his clothes, a new layer of books on his bookshelves. On Saturday, when neither of them had a show, they'd rigged up a temporary shelter of tent groundsheets in the house's desolate backyard and moved Martin's reenactment equipment into it. He kept waiting for Billy to object to this amalgamation of their households, kept trying not to take it as positive proof of forgiveness when Billy smiled instead. He wished he was absolutely certain that he knew where he stood with Billy, but he didn't really deserve that yet.

When he had moved as much as he could fit into the tiny rooms, there were other things left that he could not leave behind when the new tenants of his flat moved in. Which meant...

"Hi, Dad." Martin was sitting on the floor in front of the sofa where Billy was pretending to read a book about musical notation in the Middle Ages. He leaned back and Billy bracketed him with his long legs, so that he felt he was being hugged. He needed it right now. "How did the party go?"

"As if you would phone me to find that out. I presume you have spoken to your sister about it at least twice by now."

That's not the point, Dad. Martin thought. *I'm making small talk. It's something that people do to paper over awkward situations.* He sighed. Already this was not going well.

"All right," he said, and linked both arms around Billy's calves. Billy reached down to lay a reassuring hand on his head. "Then the reason that I'm phoning is to tell you that I'm selling my flat and moving in with somebody, and to ask if you and Mum could look after some of my things."

"You're moving in with someone?" There was the flicker of something like approval beneath his father's surprise, and Martin breathed in deep and breathed out hard to calm himself before he forced himself over the next hurdle. "Who is she? What does she do?"

The fingers on his head burrowed into his hair and stroked along his scalp calmingly. He raised his free hand and covered them, trying to absorb some of their strength. Closed his eyes. "His name's Billy, Dad. I thought it was time I should tell you that I'm gay."

Silence. Some imp of perversity prompted him to finish, "Oh, and he's unemployed."

More silence. Martin waited for a tirade, the tiny, tiny little part of himself that still hoped for acceptance and kindness faltering and dying in his chest.

Nothing on the line. "Dad?"

And then the dialling tone.

Martin took the phone away from his ear and looked at it in disbelief. He redialled and it was engaged. Or off the hook.

"What happened?" Billy leaned down to touch his shoulder, mantling over him like a hen over her chicks.

"He . . . he hung up."

"Are you all right?"

Martin didn't know. There was a kindly void in his head and his chest, where this didn't register at all, and then came anger, and he was so, so grateful for that. "Yes, I'm fine. I knew, I knew this could happen, and I said, 'Fuck him anyway.' And fuck him anyway, you know? Fuck him anyway, the old bigot. I just wanted to tell him, 'I'm not in fucking Sudan, Dad! I can be what I want here, and I'm bloody well going to. So suck it.' You know?"

"I'm sorry."

Martin scrambled off the floor and swarmed onto the sofa until he was all but sitting on Billy's lap. Since this, they had found by previous experimentation, crushed all the blood out of Billy's legs, they fell over sideways by mutual agreement, and found themselves lying side by side, tangled together in a weave of need and reassurance. "It's not your fault. I was gay before you met me, you know? I had to tell him some time. This way I can do it in your arms and that makes it easier. I'm tired of him tyrannizing over me, and if this is one way of getting rid of him, then so be it."

There was an ache in the pit of his belly that suggested he didn't actually mean that, but he ignored it. As he was trying to smile, his phone rang in his pocket.

"Dad?"

"It's Mum."

He was ashamed to say he had forgotten about her, a busy woman who loved them both distantly when she looked up from her craft projects and noticed they were there. He prayed hard she wouldn't blame herself for this, but at least she was still talking to him, right? "Hi, Mum. I'm sorry I—"

"Shh," she interrupted him. "I've just locked myself in the loo, so I've got about five minutes before he realizes I'm actually phoning you. So let me just say that I guessed years ago and that he'll come round. I presume Sheena already knows?"

"Yes, Mum." Sheena had known for the last ten years, since she caught him and Ed McMinn experimenting with kissing when they were fourteen years old.

"Well, it's good that the secret's out. That'll be one less thing for her to carry."

Martin hadn't thought of that, and it made him feel lighter, as if someone had turned up the sunlight over the golden acres of wheat outside. "Should I phone Dad back?"

"No." His mum actually laughed, fond and wise. "He's having a bit of a flap at the moment. Give him a month or so. Let him cool down. Then... I don't know. Invite us to visit your new place, perhaps, and meet him, this chap. Daddy will be too curious to resist, and he'll have remembered by then that he can't do without you."

"Yeah, right."

"He loves you very much, you know." The words came accompanied by the sound of pouring water. She was faking washing her hands. Time was running out, so he didn't say, *I know you always say that, but I haven't seen any evidence of it.* Perhaps she knew her husband better than anyone else in the world, and it was a comforting thought.

"Mum . . ." God, would he never stop crying? His eyes were leaking again as he tried to think of a way to tell her how much this little stolen phone call meant to him. "Thank you."

"Anytime, sweetie. I love you very much too."

"I love you too, Mum. Thank you."

"Shh," she said again, a little tearful herself now, by the sound of it. "What are mothers for? Speak to you soon. Bye."

"Bye," he said, but she had already rung off, leaving him still angry with his father, but with that ache in his stomach profoundly relieved.

"Are you sure you're all right?" Billy asked, slowly undoing the buttons of Martin's shirt so he could push his comforting hands inside and stroke them over Martin's skin.

Was he all right? On consideration... "I think it could have gone worse," he admitted, hope and his mother's words beginning to fill in the void over which his anger had roared. If his father came round, Martin would be ready to forgive him, like an equal, like the fellow adult that he was. Perhaps standing up to him *would* make the man realize that Martin had grown up now, that he shouldn't be treated as a child anymore. That was almost a pleasant thought.

Also pleasant was the weight of Billy's body, the long legs tangled between his, and those long talented fingers drawing music out of his lower back and his hips. "I think only my pride is hurt," he decided eventually. "And maybe you could kiss that better?"

CHAPTER
TWENTY-FOUR

The sun shone bright over Cambridge County Fair, though the wind was so cold and so brisk they'd had to double-guy all the shelters. Martin stood by his firebox, glad of the warmth on his legs, and sipped at the beaker of coffee he had told the last member of the public was holly bark boiled in goats' milk—a treatment for asthma.

They had pitched on a slight rise and could see down over the parched stubble of the field to where the young braves of Bretwalda were practising their sword craft under the admiring gaze of a couple of grannies. It was a moment out of time. The whirr of Saebriht's pole lathe provided a rhythmical accompaniment to the sound of Christine from the Early Dance Group playing something soft and plaintive on her bone whistle. The wind stretched out the flags over the camp and hummed in the throat of the dragon standard. Maybe it came from the sea, because it carried a feeling of departure, of freedom, unanchored from past or present. It carried hope.

And so did Billy, as he came striding up the beaten dirt path with his top hat on and his ragged jacket slung casually over his shoulder. He'd already taken off the face paint, looked open and reachable as he paused a moment to be sure no one was watching, then ducked under the ropes and disappeared into Martin's tent.

As always, he moved like a wild beast, an odd combination of graceful, shy, and powerful. But his smile was all human—nuanced and wry and a little bit vulnerable as he returned to the place that had rejected him before.

"Guys?" Martin raised his voice to alert the elders of his society, each watching over their own displays, knowledgeable and ready to talk to anyone who was interested. "Can I have a word?"

They came in under the canvas roof and drew close to the fire, all of them slightly dirty, with soot under their fingernails, ground in soil and mud and sweat in their garments. Even the civilians of the society, who didn't fight at all, were tougher, more capable than ordinary people. Wrapped in their cloaks, knives at their belts, surrounded by a world they'd made with their own hands . . . they were precious to him. He valued their respect, and he couldn't do this alone.

Ducking his head through the flap of his tent, he saw Billy had shucked his dancing costume and was just buckling a belt around his full-skirted Saxon tunic. They came into the work shelter together, and Martin could see the conclusions being drawn long before he opened his mouth.

"So. I think most of you were there when I had a bit of a meltdown at Hunstanton, right?"

Murmurs of assent, and he hoped also approval. The guys liked things straightforward, laid on the table without deceit. "You caught me by surprise. I said some stuff I meant, but I also said some stuff I really didn't mean."

Edith caught his eye, looked between him and Billy, meaningfully.

"Yes," he agreed, reaching out to take Billy's hand. He'd been practising, over the past two weeks, allowing himself to make little gestures of affection that couldn't be misinterpreted, but that had been in front of an uncaring public. In front of people who didn't know who he was. This time it was important, and it felt . . . it felt like maybe the bravest thing he'd ever done.

Billy squeezed his hand reassuringly, and that helped.

"So yes, I *am* going out with Billy. That's not going to change, and if you don't like it, well, frankly, you can fuck off."

He didn't want to pause, but his throat closed over breathlessness, and he had to take a moment to ease it enough to breathe in again.

No shocked looks. One or two people glanced down, picked at their hands or their shoes, but there were no overt grimaces. No laughter.

He didn't give it any time to get started. "I am going to continue with the Early Dance Group. I mentioned to some of you earlier that, far from being a threat to Bretwalda, it's actually good publicity. It's already got us some film work, which should be a nice little earner. So that's not going to stop either."

Time to put the ball firmly back in their court, give them something to think about other than his obvious inadequacies. "What this means is that I can't do quite as much as I have been doing for Bretwalda. I'm happy to carry on arranging the food and the firewood, but I can't afford to keep a car running to bring the work shelter and cooking gear, so that needs to go home with someone else. I can't carry on doing everything, so either we're going to have a meeting this evening where we're going to decide what jobs need to be done and who's going to do them or you can tell me now you don't want me to be in charge anymore, and I'll step down at once. That works for me too. I'm fine with just turning up as a grunt and letting someone else take over. But then that someone else is going to have to be one of you."

Billy's hand felt scalding in his own. He'd never felt so on show before, and for a black Viking, that was saying something. He didn't even know if he'd been forgiven yet—if he was taking a chance that might lead to him losing Bretwalda and then losing Billy anyway. But that didn't matter. (It mattered very much.) Because he'd promised. This was what he had to do to earn forgiveness, so this was what he was doing.

Then Edith smiled. "I'm sorry," she said. "We all realized, I think, that we'd been asking too much of you, and then we made fun too. I'm not surprised you were cross. We'll go away and think about this, come back this evening with some ideas. But you'll stay in charge while we make the changes? Because I think if you just left, the whole thing would fall apart, and we've only just started to get going."

The sense of relief was indescribable. He'd been prepared to leave, right now. Pack up all his stuff and go. Start again by reenacting some other historical era, maybe, though he couldn't think of one he liked as well as this. "Is that what everyone thinks?"

"You're a fucking wanker." Rolf tossed a handful of pine cones onto the fire. He made a sharp, exaggerated gesture in Billy's direction. "What d'you think this is, the nineteen fifties? You could have just fucking told us. It's not like anyone cares."

Billy watched Martin relax and gathered that that had been a more reassuring comment than it seemed to him. Even now, Martin's people weren't exactly looking at Billy himself—he existed to them as a known fact rather than a person. But that didn't matter as long as he hadn't damaged Martin's relationship with them. He was happy to be nothing more than Martin's other half in their eyes, as long as they acknowledged that he existed and that he had a claim over Martin too.

They'd returned to the doctor after his blood tests came back, and he'd been given a prescription for antidepressants, along with the warning that this was only a first try, and that finding the right combination of drugs could take a while. But so far his experience with them had been pretty good.

They hadn't taken away the despair, the voice that told him he deserved to be annihilated, that he took up too much of the world's resources by breathing and thinking and standing still. But they'd put a barrier in place between Billy and the darkness. The voice's words were muffled and distant, easier to ignore. The weight that pressed him down was easier to lift and therefore there was more energy left over to cope with the things that would once have overwhelmed all of his resources.

Often now, when he watched Martin smile or dance or deal with life in a deft combination of patience and bluntness, something new would slip across the surface of that barrier. Something better than the occasional heart-racing satisfaction of dancing, more solid than the out-of-body bliss of music. He hesitated to call it contentment, though that was the only word that came close.

Martin had done this for him—rescued him from his own demons, pulled him back from the brink of an abyss so deep it had no end. He eyed Martin's new haircut with ridiculous pleasure, itching to get his hands into it. He had loved the braids, but he loved the symbolism more. He wondered if Martin knew that his reaction to letting Billy down was to make himself into a new man, to ruthlessly cut off what he didn't like and start something new. The thought caught at Billy's heart with hooks of joy. Martin had remodelled himself for him.

He was a keeper, that was for sure.

"So I'll see you all in the morning," Martin was saying now. It made Billy smile and catch Annette's eye as she hurried up to find them. There was a show for the Early Dance Group to put on under cover in the beer tent, and after that... home.

Home, where his emptinesses had begun to be filled with Martin's things, Martin's presence. Home, where even if he did crash again, it would be with Martin's knee under his cheek as he lay on the sofa. With Martin smiling down on him as they gently squabbled about something unimportant. Martin, who had looked past the mask and seen something valuable in Billy that even Billy didn't know was there.

Martin made him wish to, strive to be real. Because, inexplicable though it might be, Martin seemed to think that when he was with Billy, he was not alone.

It was a heady experience, being seen. But if there had to be only one person in the whole world with eyes open enough to take Billy in, he was glad it was Martin.

"You ready?" Martin asked, leaning down and picking up Billy's hearpe, handing it to him. The ancient instrument had become part of Billy over the past months. He kept finding more and more in it, as if once unsilenced, once passed to a player who understood how to let it sing, it was grasping at the opportunity, leaping forward into life, blossoming and teaching him underneath his fingers.

He knew how it felt. "Yeah," he said and gave in to the impulse to lean forward and run his fingers through Martin's springy hair.

"I never asked if you liked it," Martin said quietly, as they strolled down the hill, the discordant soundscape washing over Billy, as easily ignored as air.

"I really do. But I don't think there's anything you could do to it that would put me off."

He caught a sheen of nervous sweat on Martin's forehead as Martin glanced away. Protectiveness, unfamiliar but welcome, welled up inside at the thought that what had just happened must have been harder for Martin than he thought. Stopping, he wiped Martin's face with the sleeve of his under-tunic, and then with his palms, leaving it warm and dry, and slightly downcast.

"What's wrong?"

Martin took a moment to lean his face into Billy's hand and close his eyes. They stood together in the sunshine and the scent of chimney cake and candy floss, while Billy had an uncontrollable urge to destroy whatever it was that was putting doubt on Martin's face now.

"Nothing. It's silly. I know."

"Come on," Billy wheedled, "tell me. I'm not the only one in this relationship who gets to demand to have their every whim pandered to, you know. You get to ask for things too."

Martin chuckled, but it wasn't a particularly happy laugh. "It's just . . ." He turned and began walking again towards the red-and-white marquee where they were due to perform. "You seem . . . more solid. Stronger now. On the meds, I mean. You seem more on an even keel."

Billy was not so much better that he didn't immediately think, *God, this is good-bye.* Despite everything he'd been thinking moments before, his voice still came out sharp. "And you liked me more when I was needy and dependent on you?"

Martin's eyes flicked up to meet his, dark as the night sky, dark as the universe. "No! Not that. It makes me happy when you're happy." The gaze dropped again. His mouth tugged in as if trying to keep back something bitter.

"I just . . ." He walked faster, muttering something indistinguishable at the toggles on his shoes.

"What?"

"I just think that maybe you don't need me anymore. I messed things up so badly, I don't know how you can forgive me. You deserve so much more than me, and maybe now you'll find someone who can give it to you. Someone *employed*. Someone *better*."

While they talked, the ground had gone by under their feet and now they were at the beer-tent entrance. Billy backed into one of the guy ropes to make room for the push of singlet-clad men and halter-topped women in and out of the door.

"There couldn't be anyone better for me than you," he said, earnestly, racking his brains for something poetic to say that would convince Martin. Didn't the man know he'd been forgiven a long time ago? That Billy thought he was uniquely wonderful, the centre of his universe? He tried to think how he could show Martin that, how he could tell him and be believed.

But then the compere inside announced the Early Dance Group on the microphone, and they had to hurry to Annette's side so she and Billy could tune their instruments to each other.

Martin walked out to begin his talk. His step was a fraction slow, his mouth turned down. It was clear the reassurance hadn't got through.

CHAPTER
TWENTY-FIVE

Martin dreamed of being in a Viking boat rowing over a choppy swell, and woke to find it was nine thirty in the morning and Billy was shaking his shoulder with frenetic glee. He blinked the world into focus, began to say "nnuh, what?" but Billy leaned forward and put a hand over his mouth. He shut up.

Billy's eyes were opened wide, his face shining. He handed Martin his mobile phone and mouthed, "It's the school."

That cleared Martin's head instantly. Struggling out of the duvet, he swung his legs over the side of the bed so he could take this one while sitting up. "Martin Deng."

"Mr. Deng? It's Anna Crewe at Trowbridge Academy here. I'm pleased to say . . ."

Martin bit the side of his mouth, trying to stop the squeak of anticipatory pleasure.

". . . that we were all very impressed with your interview last Monday. Unfortunately . . ."

Thank God he hadn't made a noise. It was bad news after all.

". . . we don't have a permanent place to offer you, but we would like you to come in on a temporary contract with the option of upgrading you in future if a permanent position becomes available."

No, it wasn't! It wasn't bad news. After so long trying, so many rejections, he couldn't comprehend it or believe it all at once. Was it really happening? Was he just dreaming the whole thing? Oh, who the hell cared? Why not enjoy the sensation while he could? He covered his mouth, pinched his nose closed for a moment to foil the squeak again, and managed a passable imitation of someone who was calm and together and decorously pleased.

"That's wonderful news. When would you like me to start?"

Billy frisked away like the gazelle he was and returned with a notebook and pen so that Martin could take down the details, which he did with a hand that trembled so badly from relief and joy that he half feared he would never be able to read them again.

In two weeks, as it turned out. They wanted him to start at the beginning of the new academic term, on the fourteenth of September. He barely kept the laughter out of his voice until he'd firmly and decisively accepted the position and taken down all the instructions. He rang off, dazed, threw the phone onto the bedside table, caught Billy by the back of the head and dragged him into a filthy kiss.

Getting his hands into Billy's hair, he tugged, and Billy crawled up onto the bed with him. For some reason, Billy was already dressed. But that was easily remedied, and they celebrated Martin's new job in a flurry of discarded clothes and triumphant, joyous sex.

It was a full hour later that Billy looked at his watch—which he had not bothered to take off—and said "Oh no, we'll be late!"

He rubbed his cheek and then his bruised throat along Martin's crisp new haircut, giving an exaggerated shiver of delight at the texture against his skin, then looked at Martin, side-eyed and sly.

"Late?" Martin asked, stretching the afterglow out of his limbs. "What for?"

"I arranged something to cheer you up." Billy shrugged his trousers and T-shirt back on. After a glance through the curtains, he added a flannel shirt on top and gave a rueful chuckle. "But it will probably do for a celebration instead."

He padded out to the kitchen, and Martin, still feeling expansive and obliging towards the whole world, had a very quick shower, cleaned his teeth, and was half-dressed before Billy returned with two mugs of coffee and his meds.

Billy took the pills unself-consciously under Martin's gaze. They hadn't discussed this as a ritual, and Martin would certainly have never asked for it—he would love Billy just the same if he never took the things again—but it seemed to have happened by itself. Perhaps Billy just needed Martin to see him do it, in the same way that he liked Martin noticing that he existed. Maybe it helped with some kind of placebo effect?

Billy fidgeted when he was done, bouncing on the side of the bed with his face turned away from Martin. He looked indecisive, as though the job offer, welcome though it was, had thrown a crimp in his plans. "I... uh. I don't want to overshadow the good news. I didn't know this was going to happen like this. I think." A lick of the lips and he glanced at Martin and away again. "I would have chosen a different day, if I'd known. I'm sorry."

Martin sobered, allowing his bubbling sense of relief to go off the boil, letting it just rest there under his heart like a little source of warmth. Whatever this was, it was obviously important to Billy, and Billy had done it for him. So he would damn well appreciate it to the best of his ability.

He dressed quickly: new socks, a jumper because autumn had begun to make its presence known and there was a nip in the air, but the bright-yellow one, cheerful as he felt.

"It must be a hell of a surprise if it can top the new job," he said, grinning as he shovelled down a bowlful of cereal. "I'm sure I'm going to love it. Hey..." The thought struck him because he wanted to do something nice for everyone. "Once I have some money coming in, we could install a stair lift. Get Mrs. Webb one of those mobility scooter things so she could go outside every now and again, what d'you think?"

Billy bit his already kiss-swollen lips, keeping them plump and red. He gave a wide, slightly frantic smile of approval. "I think..." He checked his watch again. "I think we really ought to go."

"What should I bring?"

"I've, um. I've done it." Billy hefted on the backpack, his eyes sliding past Martin's as he looked out of the window rather than meet Martin's gaze. Something furtive about the gesture tripped up Martin's contentment and placed the sliver of sharp ice back in his gut. What was going on?

"Okay. Lead on, then."

The bus journey to the bottom of Wednesday Hill only wound the screw tighter, Billy shifting all the way like he had a full-body rash and needed to scratch. As they walked up the footpath to Urd's well, Martin tried to think what he might have done to cause this. Was Billy worried that now he had a job he wouldn't need the support anymore?

No, that didn't make sense because he'd obviously arranged this before the job. Was he working up to letting Martin down gently? Some kind of tactful breakup plan now he didn't need Martin anymore? He'd *said* Martin was good for him, he seemed happy enough, but Martin couldn't help fretting that...

One good thing came into his life, another left. Meeting Billy, he'd lost his job. It would be poetic justice, maybe, if gaining a job meant he lost Billy. Expecting to have both at once did seem like an excess of good luck, now he thought about it. More than he deserved, perhaps. Billy had still not *said* that he was finally forgiven, after all, and he kept not daring to ask.

They reached Wednesday Keep, the hill fort, in uncomfortable silence, Martin's mood reflecting back to Billy, Billy's to him in a feedback loop of increasing uncertainty.

"Are you okay?" Billy said, coming in close to take his elbow in a gesture that never failed to warm him with its old-fashioned fifties' movie charm. He managed a smile.

"Never better. What are we up here for?"

Billy echoed it, a tiny flash of hope and mischief in his eyes. "Come on."

He led Martin to the blue plastic tent around the excavation and knocked against one of the metal poles that held it up.

"Finally!" A muddy man with spiky caramel-coloured hair lifted the flap and smiled at Billy with recognition. He gestured them inside, peering at Martin with friendly curiosity as he came. "And you must be Martin. I'm James Huntley, curator at Trowchester museum. I have oversight over this dig. How d'you do?"

Martin shook hands, slightly reassured. A dumping didn't seem to be the kind of thing one did in front of observant academics. "Hi, I'm Martin—"

"Billy's partner." James smiled, turning to lead Martin to a corner of the dig where a rectangular patch of soil had been marked out with string, divided into two plots of one metre square. They hunkered down there together. Martin noticed that the soil in one half seemed darker, softer than in the other. "Yes, I know. He told me you're keen on archaeology? You wanted to have a go?"

Martin's anxiety eased open like a mantrap, leaving him feeling bruised and shaky but free. James handed him a trowel and a brush, indicated the notepad and pen lying next to the marked-out area. "Well, I have an hour before my students arrive, so we'll go over this first square together while I show you how it's done, and then you can do the second by yourself."

He looked up at Billy. Some kind of exchange of information was made, but Martin couldn't work out what it was. "I should tell you," James went on, when Billy gave a shrug of resignation, "that we have been over the second square already, but I'm convinced it was done badly and there's something we've missed."

All this nervousness about doing something so thoughtful? Straightening up, Martin strode over to squeeze Billy tight in a relieved hug. "This is brilliant! Thank you! Is this what you were worrying about? Silly old thing! It's like a birthday—two presents at once. Thank you!"

Billy did a good job of smiling, but Martin could feel the tension all along his spine that said whatever it was that was bugging him hadn't been resolved at all. He went back to James with his delight over the surprise slightly marred by worry and puzzlement.

It was still fascinating, when James showed him how to peel down the soil, how to distinguish different shades, different textures of soil from each other. What this faint colouring of red meant, or that line of black. The bump when he hit his first object with the tip of his trowel was a full-body experience of excitement like the shock of loosing a bow.

Billy rolled up the sides of the tent around them as they worked on the first square, James showing him how to catalogue the potsherds he found, and the—"Oh, that's nice!"—the stippled twist of green material that turned out to be a broken bronze finger ring.

The light inside turned golden as he worked, almost losing himself in the fierce focus of the discipline, prevented from it only because every time he raised his head, he found Billy pacing.

There was something going on. Something more than this. What the hell was it?

"Okay," said James, as they reached the final corner of the first square. "I'm going to go light the camping stove and make us all some coffee. Why don't you get started on the second square?"

He ducked out from under the awning and walked off across the hill top, disappearing through the gate in the inner bank. His stove must be in his vehicle down in the car park.

Martin looked at Billy, who was chewing his lips again, and thought of throwing the trowel down, going over, and demanding an explanation.

But that would be a poor show of appreciation in the middle of a treat Billy had arranged. Maybe Billy was nervous because he wanted to see Martin enjoying himself and Martin wasn't. Well, he was. He was, he just wished he knew what was going on. He wished he could somehow rule out the idea that this awkwardness was the way everything ended.

Billy gave him a too-bright smile, folded his arms, turning to look out at the bowl of grassy walls around them. Martin turned to the second square, glad that it had already been dug, aware that he was too on edge to do it justice.

His heart still leapt into his mouth when he felt the thunk on the end of his trowel. Something was there. He slowed his pace, dropped his gaze, and carefully lifted the soil from around the end of it. The high sun shone slantwise against something that glittered back.

Gold. A gold edge. Some kind of design on it that looked familiar. He followed its lines along, gently, revealing the sharp side of a small gold box, with faience insets of orange and turquoise in the shape of outspread wings.

The moment he'd scraped enough soil off, he knew it was a reproduction of a box from Kush that could not have landed in this cold dark soil by accident. He dropped the trowel and unearthed it from its bed of dirt with his fingers, lifting it out.

What?

Billy must have put this here, staged the whole thing so that he would dig this out and know it couldn't have been meant for anyone but him.

He didn't . . . didn't know what to . . .

Brushing the last of the dirt from the lid, he cracked it open, looked inside. A black velvet lining, a scroll of paper. When he lifted the paper, a ring rolled out into his palm. Flat sectioned gold with chased designs of interlocking triangles. A Viking ring of the sort exchanged at a Viking wedding.

He closed shaking fingers over it and fumbled open the scroll.

You didn't seem to believe me when I said there would never be anyone better for me than you. I thought this might convince you. I love you, Martin. Marry me?

It was too much. He tucked the paper back into the box, clutched ring and box tight, and folded himself around them both, holding on while the flood of incredulous happiness threatened to sweep him away. Not dumped at all. Not dumped, but kept. Kept forever. It was too much. He was too lucky. He couldn't be ...

Billy's long arms came around him as Billy snugged up tight against his back, put his head down between Martin's shoulder blades. The touch grounded him, allowed the current of excess joy some outlet. Helped him to almost believe this was really happening.

"I'm sorry," Billy said, apologising, of course. "It seemed romantic when I thought of it. But then I couldn't stop being terrified. I don't mean to put you on the spot or pressure you, but I'm going out of my mind here. Please tell me—"

"Yes!" Martin turned and fitted himself into the spaces left by Billy's lanky form. They formed one tangled ball of limbs, and he felt sure they were so radiant together that the fucking sun was envious. "Yes, of course. Oh God, yes."

Now it was Billy's turn to give way to the borderline hysterical laughter of a man whose nerves have suddenly been detuned by joy. Martin held on to him, anchoring him as he worked his way through it, marvelling at how much thought and preparation, how much effort and stealth had gone into this. He appreciated for the first time how much Billy was capable of, now he was a little closer to well.

"Heh," he said, feeling invincible, picturing his father's face. "Well, Mum said I should wait a while and then invite my father to a family do, somewhere public where politeness would restrain him. What better than this, though—sending them invites to the wedding?"

Billy uncurled enough to give him a radiant smile, blue eyes as startlingly vivid as ever against the backdrop of summer sky. "It's a bit pointed, isn't it? You're not even a little scared of what he might say?"

Martin considered it. "No. He won't make a scene because he holds that sort of thing in contempt. Even if he hasn't come around, the worst he's likely to do is go for 'dignified in the face of tragedy.' Which I think we can cope with, don't you? At any rate, as long as I've got you, I don't give a toss about Dad's opinion. He can like it or shove off."

He leaned in for a long, appreciative kiss, and then slipped the ring on his finger, where it fitted snug and right. As they disentangled and stood up, he kept looking at it, admiring the way it shone. No, he wasn't afraid.

Just as Billy, when he was well, was clearly capable of great things, Martin, when he was happy, was going to be unstoppable. He took Billy's hand and turned to face where a coachload of tourists were beginning to trickle into the site.

"Together we're going to rock the world."

Billy shoved him with an elbow and laughed, brilliantly happy. "Or at least folk it."

Amused, Martin kissed him again, right in front of all the startled onlookers. "Folk it" was right—like the reenactors and folk dancers they were, they would do what was in their hearts and not give a damn if society thought it was weird. He really should have seen this one coming, if he'd only dared hope enough. "'Haste to the Wedding' indeed."

Explore more of the *Trowchester Blues* series at:
riptidepublishing.com/titles/universe/trowchester-blues

Dear Reader,

Thank you for reading Alex Beecroft's *Blue Eyed Stranger*!

We know your time is precious and you have many, many entertainment options, so it means a lot that you've chosen to spend your time reading. We really hope you enjoyed it.

We'd be honored if you'd consider posting a review—good or bad—on sites like **Amazon, Barnes & Noble, Kobo, Goodreads, Twitter, Facebook, Tumblr,** and your blog or website. We'd also be honored if you told your friends and family about this book. Word of mouth is a book's lifeblood!

For more information on upcoming releases, author interviews, blog tours, contests, giveaways, and more, please sign up for our weekly, spam-free newsletter and visit us around the web:

Newsletter: tinyurl.com/RiptideSignup
Twitter: twitter.com/RiptideBooks
Facebook: facebook.com/RiptidePublishing
Goodreads: tinyurl.com/RiptideOnGoodreads
Tumblr: riptidepublishing.tumblr.com

Thank you so much for Reading the Rainbow!

RiptidePublishing.com

RIPTIDE PUBLISHING

ALSO BY ALEX BEECROFT

Historical
Blessed Isle
The Crimson Outlaw
Captain's Surrender
False Colors
His Heart's Obsession
All at Sea
By Honor Betrayed
The Reluctant Berserker

Fantasy
Under the Hill: Bomber's Moon
Under the Hill: Dogfighters
Too Many Fairy Princes
The Wages of Sin
The Witch's Boy

Contemporary
Shining in the Sun

Trowchester Blues series
Trowchester Blues
Blue Steel Chain (July 2015)

ABOUT THE AUTHOR

Alex Beecroft was born in Northern Ireland during the Troubles and grew up in the wild countryside of the English Peak District. She studied English and philosophy before accepting employment with the Crown Court where she worked for a number of years. Now a stay-at-home mum and full-time author, Alex lives with her husband and two children in a little village near Cambridge and tries to avoid being mistaken for a tourist.

Alex is only intermittently present in the real world. She has spent many years as an Anglo-Saxon and eighteenth-century reenactor. She has led a Saxon shield wall into battle, and toiled as a Georgian kitchen maid. For the past five years she has been taken up with the serious business of morris dancing, which has been going on in the UK for at least 500 years. But she still hasn't learned to operate a mobile phone.

In order of where you're most likely to find her to where she barely hangs out at all, you can get in contact on:

Twitter: @Alex_Beecroft
Her blog: alexbeecroft.com/blog
Her website: alexbeecroft.com
Facebook: facebook.com/alex.beecroft.1
Facebook Page: facebook.com/AlexBeecroftAuthor
Tumblr: tumblr.com/blog/itsthebeecroft

Or to be first with news, exclusives and freebies, subscribe to the newsletter: tinyurl.com/Beecroft-Newsletter

Enjoy this book?
Find more romantic suspense at
RiptidePublishing.com!

The Two Gentlemen of Altona
ISBN: 978-1-62649-219-6

Home the Hard Way
ISBN: 978-1-62649-146-5

Earn Bonus Bucks!
Earn 1 Bonus Buck for each dollar you spend. Find out how at RiptidePublishing.com/news/bonus-bucks.

Win Free Ebooks for a Year!
Pre-order coming soon titles directly through our site and you'll receive one entry into a drawing to win free books for a year! Get the details at RiptidePublishing.com/contests.

RIPTIDE PUBLISHING

CPSIA information can be obtained at www.ICGtesting.com
Printed in the USA
LVOW07s1720100715

445789LV00005B/357/P

9 781626 492134